(The Destination)

HAPPY READING

By Clayton M. Martin

Copyright © 2001 by Clayton M. Martin.
All rights reserved. Printed in the United States of America.
No part of this publication may be reproduced, stored in
a retrieval system, or transmitted, in any form or by any
means, electronic, mechanical, photocopying, recording,
or otherwise, without the prior written permission of the author

ISBN
1-929925-92-1

10 9 8 7 6 5 4 3 2 1

Clayton M. Martin
El Destino
(The Destination)

FIRSTPUBLISH A Division of Brekel Group, Inc.
300 Sunport Ln.
Orlando, FL 32809
407-240-1414
www.firstpublish.com

Dedication

With deep devotion I dedicate this book to my son, Terry and my wife, Betty without whose assistance this book would not have been possible.

Chapter 1

On the first day of April 1821, March McCloud celebrated his birthday by setting out on the trip of a lifetime along with his wife and 12-year-old daughter, Amie. They were leaving South Carolina. Their destination would be determined by circumstances encountered along the way, but their aim was Valdosta, a village located in south Georgia.

March and his wife, Omie, both 29 years old are homeless and nearly penniless. Their future at this point is built around hope--hope that from this day forward they might, by the grace of God, be their own masters.

By way of worldly goods they own one iron bedstead, two feather ticks, three or four ragged blankets, a frayed quilt, a two-eyed heater that doubles as a cook stove, assorted pots, one cast iron Dutch oven, some tin plates and cups, assorted cutlery, two plows, an ax, one crosscut saw, one washpot, one wash tub, a two-horse wagon in reasonable condition, two mules, and a milk cow. For protection from Indians, bears, and wolves, March carries a muzzle-loading rifle. He has enough powder and lead for approximately fifty shots.

March is, or had been, a tenant farmer. Neither he nor his father had ever owned any land. He had spent his entire life working for the other man.

He had been informed three days ago by the owner of the farm that he and his family would have to vacate the shanty they had occupied for the last four years, and March would no longer be needed. The land was worn out. It would no longer sustain the growth of cotton.

Everyone knew it was just a matter of time until that would happen. Farmers and tenants alike, they were all in the same boat. Farmers couldn't pay the taxes on their lands from the meager earnings they received from their share of failing crops. Tenants couldn't support a family and mules to work worn-out land.

Maybe it was just as well; the only thing he had gained since going to work for Mr. Hastings was just enough to eat and a place that barely kept the rain out. With his meager pay and a garden to help out they had barely managed to survive.

His heart was hurting for his wife and child, but what could he do? He had been ordered to leave, and leave he must.

Omie's folks were in Kansas. Omie sent them a letter telling them they were moving to Valdosta, Georgia. She would write when they were settled.

Last night they said their good-byes to March's kin and the few people they knew; now it was time to go. March threw the remainder of their plunder on the wagon, including a crate with six hens and a rooster, climbed up, and with a last look called to the mules, "Come up there now." Omie sat stoically looking straight ahead. Amie followed along behind the wagon to ease the load.

From where they lived on the southern edge of South Carolina to the Georgia border was just a few miles. Once inside Georgia, March intended to turn to the southwest and head for Valdosta. He had heard there might be work for good hands in the cotton fields. March didn't like to brag, but he knew his cotton as well as any man.

He hadn't raised a good crop lately, but that wasn't his fault. When the ground was worn-out and the rains don't come, well, there just wasn't much a man could do except pray and hope. March certainly had done plenty of both lately. Neither had done any good. So here he was with three dollars cash money, a wife and child, and not much else.

Why, Omie didn't even have any snuff. All he had in the way of tobacco were a few hanks of "ginny bush"-- tobacco leaves rolled and twisted together with a little molasses poured on to keep them moist. It made pretty good chewing but was hard to smoke. When they come to a store they will stop and get Omie some snuff and maybe a little tobacco for his pipe. Amie did dip some snuff, but she wasn't bad about it yet. It shore was a pleasure to have a little snuff and tobacco, especially at the end of a hard day.

At mid-morning, March stopped the wagon and let the mules blow. They nibbled a little grass growing near the road. Omie jumped down and stretched her legs. She grabbed the dipper attached to the water barrel on the side of the wagon and took several thirsty gulps. When she was through drinking, she handed the dipper filled with water to Amie, and she in turn gave it to March.

March wiped his brow and said, "The mules and cow shore could do with a drink too. Soon as we find a place we'll let them fill up."

When they started again Omie did the driving; this time March followed behind. This would be the routine from now on. Sometimes two would walk.

March sifted his life over and over, trying to decide if he could have done better by his wife and daughter. Life was shore hard, that was a fact. When he thought on it, why, he was about as well off as just about anybody else. His Pa had been a sharecropper. Look at him--he worked himself to death and died poor as a church mouse.

It looked as if March would end up the same way. It surely didn't make a man feel good about the future. "I reckon hit could be worse;" March mused softly to himself, "if all the children Omie carried had lived there would be six of us now. I don't know if I can keep the *three* of us from starving. Well, I'll just have to leave hit in God's hands 'cause I shore cain't do nothing about hit."

Along toward the middle of the day they came to a creek. March stopped the wagon to let the animals drink and rest awhile. Omie stiffly alighted from the wagon and promptly sent Amie to the creek for a bucket of fresh water.

When Amie returned March had the mules unhitched and was leading them to drink.

When they had drunk their fill he led the mules to a place where they could graze. He staked each mule on a long rope, then did the same for the cow.

As he was returning to the wagon, Omie had gotten out some cold corn pone that was left from breakfast along with a few pieces of bacon that she divided between them.

"I believe I want just a little syrup on this pone, Omie, then I'll be plumb satisfied," March said looking at Amie to see if she wanted some too.

Amie said, "I reckon I'm just too sad to eat very much. I'd shore a'heap rather be back to home than where we's at right now. Wouldn't you, Ma?"

Omie just looked at her.

March said, "Let's get in the shade; maybe we can take us a little nap 'fore we get started again."

Omie woke up when she heard the jingle of harness as March hitched the mules to resume their journey. "March, hit's mighty hot, I hope we don't kill them mules."

"We'll take hit slow and stop if they get too sweaty, don't worry none. Tonight maybe we can camp at the old sawmill. At least there will be plenty of wood for a fire, and there's a spring right near. I reckon the animals will have to eat wiregrass tonight if they can find some. What we having fer supper, Omie?"

"More pone and slab meat. Maybe soon we'll come upon some wild greens. Tomorrow if we see anything fitting to eat you can shoot hit. I shore would admire a big old soft-shell turtle, wouldn't you?"

"I shore would, Omie. You shore can cook them good. I ain't never had enough of them turtles; hit seems to me. 'Course now, Amie don't like them old turtles so we don't have to fix none for her. Ain't that right, Amie?"

"Shoot no, that ain't right. I can eat just as many as you can and a heap more too. Ma, you got any snuff?"

"No, Amie, you know I ain't got no snuff. I'd shore like a dip myself; seems a body do get along a whole heap better with a little snuff now and again. Get you a chaw of that ginny bush and make do with that."

It was nearly sundown when they came to a sawdust pile where a sawmill once stood. They pulled the wagon under a big oak tree for the night.

March unhitched the team and took them to drink. Then he staked them for the night. Amie scurried off searching for firewood to prepare the evening meal. Omie lugged the bucket to the spring for water just as the whippoorwills started calling.

When Omie returned with a bucket of cold spring water Amie already had the fire going. "Ma, hit shore is lonesome to hear them old whippoorwills a'calling. I do wish we could go back home, don't you?"

"Amie, I shore do. I tell you, one of these days we are a'going to have us a nice place of our own, then ain't nobody going to run us off no more. No, Siree Bob!"

"You reckon so, Ma?"

"Amie, when we get to wherever we's a'going and your Pa gets a good job, why hit won't be no time a'tall till we'll have our own place. You just wait and see. Pass me that cornmeal and that big spider, might just as well cook enough fer breakfast too. Tomorrow, honey, you keep your eyes open fer some greens. A body cain't live without something green. March, oh March, come on in. I've got supper near bout done; you hear?"

"Yeah, Omie, I hear you, I'm so hongry I could eat a fried mule and a acre of collard greens. Here's what little milk I got tonight."

"Well, don't go getting no ideas about them mules, unless yore figuring on walking to Valdosta. A'fore you set down, thank the Lord fer these here vittles we's got. While you're at hit, ask him to start looking for us a house too."

"Omie, ain't he always took good care of us? But I reckon hit won't hurt to remind him again. *Lord, we are just three poor children in the wilderness who cain't do for ourselves. Lord: We just throw ourselves on yore tender mercy and ask you to care for us as you did the children on their rambles in the desert. Lord, we got some vittles, and we can sleep under the wagon, please take care of the mules as they's all we got to pull this wagon. In a short time, Lord, we are going to be in a place which we don't know nothing about, so will you please show us the way, and we shore do thank you. Amen.*"

March said, "I reckon we made about twelve or fourteen miles today, so we got a pretty good start. God only knows how many more miles to where we're a'going, or what's going to be in our way. Wish we had some greens with this pone."

After supper they sat for a while reliving the day and listening to the night sounds. They could hear the mules cropping grass and knew that they were content. The cow bellowed softly and lay down for the night.

March looked up into the sky filled with stars and wondered what tomorrow would bring. "We better go to bed if we're a'going to get an early start. Shore hope the weather stays good," he said.

Toward morning March was awakened by the wind in the trees. It started blowing softly at first, then harder. It was starting to get cold too. Soon the first drops of rain began to fall. March jumped to his feet to search for a quilt and the other half of the tarpaulin that covered the wagon. Omie and Amie slept through it all. March thought to himself, "Poor things, they're plumb tuckered out. Well, it ain't long till morning."

When water began to leak into their bed they jumped up. By now it had turned much colder, and the rain was falling heavier. The wind was blowing the deluge of rain so hard that March had a hard time starting a fire.

Using the tree to keep some of the rain off, he finally got it going. He put water on to boil to make sassafras tea. "Wish we had some grounds, ain't had no coffee this blessed year so fer;" he muttered, "a body ought to have some coffee to start out the day. Omie, reckon you could make us some flapjacks this morning? I feel like I could eat bout forty."

"I reckon so, but we ain't got much flour left, so's we got to be sparing. Hunt up that jug of syrup. Amie, roll out and hurry to the creek fer a bucket of fresh water, and mind you, get it upstream from where them mules have been a'drinking."

Amie said, "Are we moving on in this rain? I'd a'heap rather just set by the fire and keep warm."

"I reckon we can stay as warm and dry a'going as we can a'setting. Hurry with the water now. I need it fer them 'jacks. March, you find that syrup?"

"It's setting under the wagon. I'm going to check on the mules. I won't be gone long."

When March returned, Omie had a plate of flapjacks ready for him. He poured on a batch of syrup and began to eat.

"These here 'jacks do taste good on a morning such as this. With enough of these, why, I reckon a body could go all day long without another mouthful. We're purty near into Georgia. The sooner we get started the more miles we're a'going to get behind us."

As soon as Omie cleaned the dishes and washed the spider, Amie had the beds rolled up and stored in the wagon. Omie looked around for March and saw him coming back with the mules and the cow. Soon he had the mules hitched, and they rolled out.

Omie drove and March and Amie slogged along behind the wagon. The road was muddy and slick with red clay and walking was slow and tiresome.

March had been this way one time before, but he couldn't remember whether they were on the right road or not. He would just have to ask the first person they saw for directions. If he remembered right, they ought to come pretty near making it all the way to Savannah today.

Amie had never been to a place as large as Savannah. March wanted her to see it. She might never have another chance. Omie had never been to Savannah either.

It was plodding, bone weary going for the mules. The road now was just a dim trail and not quite as muddy as before. March put Amie to driving the wagon, and he and Omie followed along behind. "Omie, if we can find the way, we're a'going to stop for a little while in Savannah. We need to get you some snuff and me some tobacco. We best not ferget to get flour neither. What you think of that?"

"I'd shore like to see Savannah. I know Amie would too. But we cain't afford to spend no money, 'cept maybe for a little flour and tobacco. We ain't got but three dollars, and Lord knows when we'll get any more. We had ought to get a little sack of corn for them chickens too, but I reckon we can ketch enough bugs and grasshoppers to keep them alive."

"Yeah, I know we're mighty short on cash. Maybe we should of sold the mules and wagon and walked to Valdosta. You cain't never tell though, we might need the mules to tend a little patch 'fore we get some work to do. Besides, you cain't be no sharecropper without a mule and plow."

They stopped at noon to rest the mules and to eat a bite. The rain was falling steadily now, and it was getting much colder with every passing minute. The month of April is always an unpredictable time of the year. One day hot, the next day cold as all get out.

March was beginning to worry that they had taken the wrong road. The one they were on seemed dim and untraveled. "Well, if we don't see a house purty soon, we'll have to turn back," he said.

As they were loading the wagon to resume their trek, March thought he heard a dog barking in the distance. Holding up his hand for quiet, he listened intently for a moment, then said, "Omie, you hear that dog?"

"Yeah, March, I hear him, sounds like he's purty close. Let's hurry up and see if we can find him. Come on, Amie." As they hurried forward the barking became louder, and soon they were in sight of a shanty hidden amongst the trees.

The dog they had heard barking was under the porch. A man with a gun was standing in the doorway. March stopped the mules and called to him. "Good day to you, Sir. I reckon me and my family are lost. Can you tell us how to get to Savannah?"

"Well, I reckon I can. It's a right smart way from here. Best way is to turn around and go back 'bout four or five miles and take the right fork. That'll take you right into Savannah. Where you folks from?"

"We be the McClouds from Pine Top. That's in South Carolina. 'Course, I reckon you know that? This here is my wife, Omie, and this is our little girl, Amie. We are a'heading to south Georgia or maybe Florida, or any place a body can find work. We done right well yesterday, but the rain has got us slowed up a mite today. You mind if we get a drink and rest the mules a little?"

"Not a'tall. Y'all step down and come on in. My name is Pearson; folks call me Jack. This ain't much of a place, but I call it home. That's old Rome, the best ketch dog there ever was."

"Jack, we shore are obliged to you. Folks call me March."

"Mr. McCloud, if you don't mind me a'saying so, you folks look like yore near 'bout drowned and 'bout froze too. Come on in this here house and warm yore self up."

"Call me March. We're much obliged to you, Jack. We're about wore out. How far did you say it was to Savannah?"

"You ain't gonna get to Savannah today, even if'n you start now. With this rain a'falling, hit'll be getting dark 'fore long. Tell you what, unhook them mules and put them in that little pasture out back, along with yore cow. You folks can stay here fer the night and get a early start tomorrow. 'Course, you'll have to sleep in the corncrib. Better than sleeping on the ground though."

"If hit won't put you out too much, I believe we'll take you up on that. Maybe we could do a little cooking in the smokehouse, if that would be all right?"

"That's fine. Can I ask you folks how come you're moving?"

"Land over to Pine Top is wore out. Mr. Hastings, he was the man I was sharecropping for, said hit cost more to plant it than he could get from it so we would have to move. Said he might sell and move to Florida or som'mers else hisself."

"You women folks come on in. March and me will unhitch the mules and unload the wagon. March, I shore would like a little taste of milk if that old cow of yore'n don't mind. Been a spell since I tasted any."

"Jack, she don't give much, but you're plumb welcome to what there is. Amie will milk her after a while."

When Jack and March got the wagon unhitched and unloaded, they turned the mules out into a little patch behind the house and then hurried inside. It felt real good in Jack's snug little cabin standing near the roaring fireplace. Steam poured from their clothes as they dried. Jack said, "I got a big pot of stew that's been a'cooking most all day, I would consider it right neighborly if y'all would help me eat hit up. If'n you don't, old Rome will just have to eat hit all by hisself. What you say?"

"That sounds mighty fine to me. How about hit, Omie, Amie?"

Amie said, "Boy, do hit ever, I'm so hongry I could eat a fried mule and a acre of collard greens."

"Don't pay her no mind, Mr. Jack; she just picked that up from her Pa," Omie said.

After they ate their fill of stew and warmed up, they spent the rest of the day swapping stories. Jack told them he used to be a farming man himself, and the same thing happened to him as had happened to them. "Then I went to trapping. Didn't last long. Had a accident. Left me almost totally crippled. I been here fer the last two years, just living off the land."

March asked, "What kind of accident did you have?"

"Well, hit was like this: I had a trap set fer an old bear that had been killing my hogs that me and old Rome had caught and were fattening up. I made a hole in a log and put some honey in it. That old bear came along and put his paw into that hole to get hisself some honey. What he didn't know was that I had driven some nails into that log a'slanting down into hit. When he got a handful of honey and started to take out his paw them nails caught him. Try as he would, he couldn't get his paw out. Well, I guess you know he was one mad bear. When me and old Rome found him, he was crazy to get away. Rome jumped him and started a'biting him. That made him worse. I had left my gun to home, and all I had was my ax. Rome was a'biting him, and that bear was trying to knock him into South Caroline. I got close and was 'bout to chop him in the head when he tore loose and come fer me as quick as a cat. He must have knocked me ten feet with his first blow. My ax went one way, and I went t'other way. 'Fore I hit the ground good that bear was on me again. He commenced to scratch and bite me all over. I knowed my time had come fer he was mad crazy and foaming at the mouth. He was a'making the worst noise a feller ever heered. He had done bit my arm mostly in two pieces. He was a'trying to get my head into his mouth when old Rome lit into him again. Well, he quit biting me and took out after Rome. Old Rome warn't scared of that bear. Well, Sir, that bear made a swipe at Rome and knocked him a'flying. Rome hit the ground, and I just knowed fer shore that he was kilt, but he warn't; he got up and run from that bear and led him right on away from me. I reckon if he hadn't I shore enough would be deader than a door nail now. I managed to get home though. Two days later a feller stopped and found me. He carried me to his house and took care of me 'till I got able to care for myself. As you can see, I ain't got but one good arm and one good leg. I owe my hide to old Rome. I wouldn't take a million dollars fer him."

"Jack, that's some story. Hope you got all them bears. I shore would hate to wake up with one a'looking to do that to me! Come on, girls, I guess we better get to bed; hit'll be a long day tomorrow."

Chapter 2

At first light March crawled out of his warm bed, hitched the wagon and was ready to go as soon as Omie and Amie loaded on the bedding. Jack pointed out a short cut through the woods to the main road, "Just head about south, southwest till you hit the plain road. That'll take you into Savannah."

They said their good-byes and headed into the woods making their own road. Sure enough, exactly as Jack said, they soon came to the main road. Just as the sun was going down they arrived in Savannah.

March persuaded the owner of a stable to allow them to spend the night in the hayloft in return for feeding and watering the stock. He even managed to get a little hay for the mules and cow.

The stable was in the middle of town, so after the wagon was unhitched and the team cared for, March suggested they walk about and see as much as they could before going to bed.

Savannah was filled with people of all nationalities. Omie and Amie understood hardly a word they heard. For Amie especially, it was a wonderful experience being in a large town for the very first time. The stores were filled with goods from all parts of the world. Amie had never seen so many goods in a store before. There were lots of eating places, with most of them filled to capacity. March felt badly not having any money to spend.

It had been a long, hard day as they headed for the stable. March checked on the mules one more time while Amie milked the cow. Omie made their beds in the hayloft on piles of hay, and they turned in for the night.

As Amie lay in the fragrant hay she made a vow to herself, "One day when I'm rich, we'll come to Savannah and stay in the finest hotels and eat in them fancy cafes."

It seemed just a few minutes had gone by when March shook her awake. Tenderly he said to Amie, "Time to get up, honey. We got to get started."

While March was loading the wagon and hitching the team, Omie and Amie walked along the dock to look at the ships. Amie had never seen anything larger than a rowboat, and she couldn't believe how large they were.

"How do they paddle a boat big as that?" Amie asked.

"They don't paddle them, honey. The wind blows them where they want them to go."

"Oh, that ain't so. Ma, how could the wind do that?"

"They have things called sails, and as the wind blows against them, that makes the ship go."

"What's a sail, Ma?"

"They look like big blankets, and they pull them up high on the ships with ropes. The wind fills them just like hit fills your Pa's shirt on the clothesline. Look, Amie, down the river, there comes a ship, and hits sails are up! See, how the wind fills em up, and the ship is moving all by hitself?"

"Ma, if I hadn't seen hit fer myself, I wouldn't believe hit. Where do all them ships come from, and where do they get all the stuff they got on them?"

"They come from all over the world, and the stuff that's on them comes from all over the world, too. I 'spect we better get on back. Yore Pa will be ready to go by now."

"Ma, if we had one of them ships, hit would be a whole lot easier than a wagon, wouldn't hit?"

"Hit purely would, 'cept you cain't go through the woods with a ship."

March was standing by the wagon when they got back and he said, "I was beginning to think y'all had got on one of them ships and left me all alone."

"They shore are purty. When we get rich can we come back to Savannah and ride on one?" Amie asked.

"When we get rich, we'll come back and be just as big as anybody. We'll ride on one of them ships just as much as you want, and we'll eat in them fancy cafes. Feller ask me if I wanted a job on one of them ships, too."

"Pa, did you take it?"

"No, Siree Bob, I said I ain't a'going nowhere without my women folks, but I thanked him just the same. Load on up now. We best be going."

Just as Amie started to scramble up on the wagon a dog came from the stables and ran up to her wagging his tail. Amie couldn't believe her eyes. "Pa, look-a-here who's followed us; why hit's old Rome!"

March sprung down and looked for himself. "Glory be, hit shore is. He must have followed us yesterday, and we never even knowed he were here."

"What we a'going to do with him, Pa? Can we keep him?"

"Well, no, Amie, he ain't our dog."

"What we gonna do with him then, Pa?"

"I don't rightly know. Hit's a fer piece back to Jack's place, but I don't want to leave him here. I know that Jack cain't hardly get along without him."

Omie said, "They ain't but one thing to do. We's got to take him back. Jack was nice to us, and in a way hit's our fault that old Rome left home."

"But, Omie, hit's a whole day back there and then a whole day back here again."

"I know, I know, but if'n he were our dog we shore would want him back. Ketch him, Amie, and tie him to the wagon. The sooner we get started, the sooner we'll get him home and get on with our trip."

Amie caught Rome and tied him to the wagon, and they started back to Jack's place.

When they got a short distance out of Savannah they untied Rome. He followed along just like he was their dog.

Late that evening when they were just a few miles from Jack's house, suddenly Rome put his nose to the ground and with a yelp took out into the woods. March and Amie both tried to call him back, but he just ignored them. The last they saw of him he was bounding over a huge log.

"What we a'gonna do now?" Omie asked.

"We ain't too fer from Jack's. We'll go on and let him know what happened."

When they came in sight of Jack's place he was out back trying to chop some wood. He looked up and said with a smile, "I see that you folks couldn't stay away from old Jack's cooking. Get down and come in. March, y'all get lost?"

"No, Jack, we found Savannah all right. When we got up this morning to leave, why there was old Rome just as purty as you please. I reckon he followed us; we just didn't know hit."

"Bless my soul, folks, I shore am sorry you had to come all this way on account of him, but I'm glad to have him back. Don't know what I'd do without him. I'm much obliged to you. Where is he?"

"About three, four miles back he suddenly struck a trail of some kind. The last we saw of him he was high tailing it fer parts unknown. We tried to call him back, but he never paid no attention to us."

"Sometimes he's that a'way when he strikes a fresh scent, reckon I'll have to go hunt him. You folks get down and unload your plunder; you cain't go no place this time of a day. March, I would be obliged if you would go with me and show me where Rome left the road."

"All right, let me get the mules and cow staked out and watered, then I'll be ready."

"I'll give you a hand. In the meantime, the women folks can make themselves to home. Miss Omie, maybe you and Miss Amie can cook us a mess of something to eat while we're gone. Just go on in and use whatever you can find. I ain't got much in the way of vittles, but they's a pot of beans I cooked, and you'll find some side meat in the smokehouse."

Omie said, "Don't y'all worry none; me and Amie will have you something to eat when y'all get back."

March and Jack shouldered their guns and started out for where Rome was last seen. After about two miles, Jack said, "Let's cut into the woods. Maybe we'll be able to hear him pretty soon."

About an hour later Jack motioned for March to stop. "Let's set a spell and just listen."

In a few minutes they heard Rome in full cry. He seemed to be coming their way. "I believe Rome is trailing a bear."

"How can you tell?"

"I have set and listened to that hound so much, I can read his mind. That's a bear fer shore."

Rome continued to come toward them. Suddenly his "trail" voice turned into a "treed" voice. Jack jumped up and said to March, "Come on, March, old Rome has got him up a tree fer shore and certain!"

Jack led the way. For a man that was crippled, he sure set a fast pace. As they hurried along, Jack let out with a cry of encouragement to Rome, "Yeeee-whoooo, Rome, get'em, boy." Old Rome heard Jack, for he let out with a series of deep barks, "Oooh, oooh, ooh, ooh!"

That encouraged Jack to keep up his hollering, "We's a'coming, Rome, get'm boy."

March was hard pressed to keep up, the brush kept tearing at his clothes. The limbs Jack pushed out of his way kept slapping March in the face.

Jack continued encouraging Rome, "Whoooo weeeee, set on'm, Rome; we's a'coming."

When they got to Rome, he was running round and round a big oak tree. Near the top sat a big old bear. The saliva from his mouth was dripping to the ground. He was growling to beat the band and shaking the tree.

Jack fell on Rome and hugged him. He said a lot of baby talk to him and praised him for treeing the bear. "Rome, I shore missed you whils't you were gone, you old devil. I's glad yore back and got us a bear, too! Whooo-eeeee!"

"March, is you ever shot a bear?"

"No, I ain't."

"Well, we're a'going to remedy that. Shoot that rascal right in front of his shoulder, he ought to hit the ground dead."

March said, "S'pose he don't?"

"Then you better be prepared to high tail hit out of here."

"You shore do make a feller feel full of confidence, Jack."

March took careful aim, and when he pulled the trigger the bear came crashing down. As soon as the bear hit the ground Rome piled on top of him. Old Rome made the fur fly.

For a minute Jack kept his gun leveled at the bear just to make sure he didn't get up. "March, you shore laid him out as purty as you please and yore fust one, too. I'll stay here with Rome and start skinning this rascal if you'll go home and get yore wagon. We'll have some bear fer supper too, if yore woman will cook it."

March hurried home to get the wagon while Jack stayed and did the skinning. When March returned they loaded the bear and Rome into the wagon and headed for home. Jack sat in the back with Rome and stroked his head and scratched his ears, all the while talking baby talk to him.

Jack sliced a few choice cuts from the bear and gave them to Omie to fry for their supper. He said the largest portion of the bear would go into the washpot to make lard. "Hit makes the best biscuits that you ever did eat, Miss Omie. We'll have some fer breakfast."

After supper they talked a long time before going to bed. Amie told Jack all the exciting things she saw in Savannah. When they were talked out, they turned in. They needed to get an early start tomorrow.

Chapter 3

Next morning March said to Jack, "I want to thank you fer letting me shoot that bear and fer them good bear steaks. Yore right about that bear grease, too. Hit do make some mighty fine biscuits. Now, we better be a'going. Else we'll have to move in with you and help finish that bear."

"March, I shore have enjoyed y'all being here with me, and yore welcome to come anytime and stay as long as you want to. I'm much obliged to y'all fer bringing Rome home, too. If you ever come this way again, you be shore to stop and visit with me."

They waved goodbye and started for Savannah again.

It was late evening when they came near to Savannah. They camped across the river but didn't go into town.

Early the next morning without taking time to eat breakfast, they resumed their trip where they had left off. When they reached Savannah, it was still cold and threatening rain. Soon they were swallowed up by the unsettled land. A light drizzle settled in. It wasn't long before they were soaked to the skin and freezing from the cold. March hated the bad weather on account of Amie and Omie, but there wasn't a thing he could do about it.

They plodded on until about eleven o'clock. March decided he had to stop, get something to eat and warm up. Starting off without any breakfast made his belly growl in a mighty big way. As soon as March came to a huge oak tree he stopped the wagon under it to get out of the rain. He unhitched the team for a rest and a drink from a puddle of water beside the road. He then staked the animals for a bite to eat.

"Y'all get down, we'll build a fire so's we can get warm. I 'spect we ought to eat a little something too; I'm starved."

Amie and Omie slid down from the wagon and soon had a fire going. Omie put on a pot of cornmeal mush for their dinner. "Hit ain't much, but hit'll keep body and soul together 'til we can do better. Amie, throw some of them small 'taters in that fire. Maybe they'll have time to get done 'fore we go, or we can eat them later."

"Ma, them chickens has laid two eggs. You want me to get them and let's cook them?"

"Bless my soul, Amie, I shore do. Two ain't much, but I'll just scramble them. Hit'll be a little taste for each of us. Your Pa will be surprised. Won't he?"

"I 'spect so, Ma."

March came up with a big grin on his face and said, "Lookee here what I found a'crawling along side of the road. A big old gopher. I reckon you want me to throw him in the wagon, don't you, Omie?"

"No, hurry up and dress him out, we'll have him fer dinner. He'll go mighty fine with this pot of mush. Amie, save the eggs till we get enough to have a big bait."

"How we a'gonna keep them from breaking, Ma?"

"Put them in the cornmeal. Hurry up with that gopher meat, March. The grease is just about hot."

"I'm a'hurrying just as fast as I can. I'm hongry too."

After eating they took a short rest, then moved on in spite of the rain and cold. They passed one or two houses, but no one seemed home so they kept moving. Late in the evening they met a man riding a horse. He gave them directions to the next village.

Just before dark they came to a creek. March decided this was a good place to make camp. He unhitched the team and staked them on some good grass after watering them. Omie had a fire going and was frying side meat. She had mixed a pone of cornbread in the Dutch oven and set it on the coals to bake. The sweet potatoes Amie had put in the ashes earlier in the day were now put back under some hot coals to finish cooking.

As soon as the bread finished cooking, Omie called them to come and eat. Immediately after taking the bread from the Dutch oven, Omie refilled it with dried peas along with a chunk of side meat. She banked the fire around it to "slow cook" all night. That would be their noon meal tomorrow along with the leftover pone, if there was any.

The rain had about ended. They were hopeful the sky would clear and warm up. Their beds were still damp and would be uncomfortable until they could dry them. Omie decided she had better make some more pone. They had eaten all the other. This time she made it in the skillet and placed it on the coals to fry.

March went to check on the team. They had been snorting and restless. March knew something was bothering them. He picked up a pine knot from the fire to show the way. He checked his gun to make sure it was ready for action. The mules were tugging on their ropes and huffing when March arrived.

He held the pine knot high over his head as he searched the bushes near where the mules were tied. March saw two enormous yellow eyes glaring at him.

Resting his rifle on a limb while holding the pine knot high, he aimed between the eyes and slowly pulled the trigger. Omie jumped when she heard March shoot.

Presently he came to the fire, dragging something behind him. It was a big panther. It had been stalking the mules and would no doubt have killed one of them if March hadn't shot him.

"What'cha gonna do with him, March? We cain't eat that varmint."

"Reckon I could skin him out and maybe trade the skin fer something? I'd hate to chunk it away."

"Hit'd make a purty rug fer the floor, but we ain't got no way of preserving hit; ain't got no floor neither," Amie observed.

March skinned the panther and rolled the hide with a little salt so it wouldn't spoil until he could maybe trade or swap it for something. Then he put the skin in the wagon. Once the pone was cooked and more sweet potatoes added to the ashes to cook overnight along with the peas, they made their beds and fell asleep listening to the frogs in the nearby creek.

March was up early as usual. After caring for the animals and staking them on some good grass, he noticed a swirl in the water. Perhaps, he could catch some fish. Unrolling his fishing line that he always kept handy, he cut himself a small, thin tree for a pole.

With a piece of rag for bait, he eased to the bank and cast up under a bush. He drew his line back with short jerks. Before you could say "Jack Robinson" he had a good size bass flopping beside him. He caught two more along with a big Jack fish. He decided that was enough for breakfast and maybe for dinner, too.

He carefully rolled and stored his fishing line, then cleaned the fish in the creek. He came strolling into camp as Omie was saying to Amie, "Wish we had more than two eggs, I could eat a bunch this morning."

"What are we going to have, Ma?"

"Flapjacks, I reckon, but we got to be sparing on that flour."

March chimed in, "Why don't you just cook us a mess of fish?"

"I would if we had some."

March had been hiding them behind his back and handed them to her saying, "Yore wish is my command, Ma'am. Here they are."

"Now, if we just had some coffee."

"One wish at the time, if you don't mind."

It was still cold, but thank goodness the rain had quit. They loaded the wagon and with March and Omie walking behind they rolled out. There was supposed to be a store and a couple of houses in a place called Lark not too far from where they had camped. There they hoped to trade the panther skin for a few supplies.

Noon came and passed. They still hadn't seen a living soul. Omie broke out the fish left over from breakfast; and these with a sweet potato made lunch.

As the sun began to set, they began to look for a likely place to camp. "Omie, you reckon we took the wrong road? I ain't seen nary other one, have you?"

"Not unless you call that pig trail a road, I ain't."

"Maybe we ain't come fer enough. We ain't been making too good a time on account of all that water a'standing everywhere. We spent a'heap of time getting across that creek, too."

Omie replied, "Well, I'm too tired to care much. Let's find a place and stop fer the night."

"Amie, pull them mules to a stop along side that old dead tree; we'll cut it up for firewood," said March.

"Don't see no water, Pa."

"We'll have to use from the barrel and give them chickens a drink, too."

"Omie, what's fer supper? Any more of that gopher?"

"Looks like peas and what's left of that pone with a sweet 'tater."

"Suits me. How about you, Amie?"
"Any old thing suits me, Pa."

After supper Omie filled the Dutch oven with lima beans and banked the pot with coals. She mixed a pone and set the spider on the coals to heat. When the pan was hot, she poured the cornmeal mixture in. It sizzled and popped for a minute, then settled down to cook emitting a special aroma while it browned in a little bacon grease. Just before they went to bed, March put several sweet potatoes in the ashes and covered them. In the morning they would be done.

Several times during the night they were awakened by the howling of wolves. The animals were picketed nearby, so March wasn't worried. After a hurried breakfast, they packed and were on their way when 'Old Sol' peeked up over the trees.

Chapter 4

About ten o'clock they came to the store they were looking for. March stopped the team and went inside. He wasn't in the store very long before he came back and told Omie to go and tell the owner what she wanted. "He give me a dollar and fifty cents for the hide," March said with a smile.

Omie and Amie got down and went inside to get the supplies while March drove the mules to a well in the back of the store and watered them. When he was through, he drove back to the front of the store. Omie was waiting with their supplies in a gunny sack. "What all did you get?" March asked.

"I got a little piece of side meat, a peck of cornmeal, a half gallon of syrup, five pounds of beans, five pounds of flour, and a plug of tobacco fer you."

"Did you get anything fer you and Amie?"

"Yeah, I got us a box of snuff, and the storekeeper give Amie five jaw breakers."

"Well, I'm right satisfied. I shore do hope we run into some more of them old panthers," March said.

They decided they wouldn't stop for dinner, but would drive till sundown and take supper instead. Each had a sweet potato and a drink of water. The animals drank from a puddle beside the road and were allowed to nibble when they came to a fine patch of grass. March had his first chew of store-bought tobacco since before leaving Pine Top. Omie and Amie both had a lip full of snuff and seemed to be pleased with themselves. Amie was enjoying a jaw breaker at the same time.

March asked, "Amie, how do you manage to swaller that candy without swallering snuff too?"

She replied, "I just swaller and hope fer the best."

"You best quit dipping that nasty old stuff. Hit's a'gonna rot your teeth out. Then ain't nary man a'gonna want to marry you."

Amie giggled and said, "I ain't a'studying nary man, Pa."

Omie said, "She better not be a'studying nary man."

"Well, Omie, you were a'studying men the first time I seen you. You shore give me a big look every time I come by yore house," March said with a wink at Amie.

"Well, I must admit that you shore did look purty a'setting on that big fine horse," said Omie with a shy smile.

"Wish I had him now to ride 'stead of having to walk."

Amie said, "Don't you worry none, Pa. When I get rich I'm a'going to buy as many horses as you and Ma want."

Along toward evening they came to a place where water covered the road. March had been warned by the store owner he would likely find the creek flooded and impassable. In that case, they would just have to wait for the creek to go down which might take as long as three or four days. This would give them a chance to rest up and dry everything out. Besides, the mules could use a rest and a chance to regain their strength. March noticed a good place just a short way back that was high and dry with lots of deadwood scattered about. It would be easy to collect for the fires.

They turned around and drove back. Omie stopped the wagon under a shade tree. March unhitched the team and took them to a little spring for water before staking them and the cow on a good patch of grass. After rolling in the dirt, the mules settled down to feed.

March took the ax and began to cut firewood. Amie carried it to where Omie had built a fire. Then she prepared supper while March and Amie continued to stack up firewood. When Omie called them to supper, after a long day without dinner, they were hungry as wolves.

Supper over, March cut a chew of tobacco for himself and leaned back against a tree to enjoy it. Amie and Omie filled their lips with snuff before doing the dishes. It felt good to lean back with a good chew and a full stomach with nothing to do but talk and listen to the night sounds. In the distance the owls were calling to each other. Close by a whippoorwill was sending his lonesome message out into the dark. From far away one answered. They were all contented, now that the rain had stopped. The cold seemed to be moderating some as well.

"March, how long you reckon hit'll take fer that creek to go down?" Omie asked.

"I ain't got no way of knowing. The feller at the store said it might take several days."

"He say if there was any other way to go?"

"Not if we want to go to Spencer. That's the only way to get to where we want to go--Valdosta."

"If we were a'riding now, why we could just take out through the woods and make our own road, but then we might get losted and wind up no telling where. Guess we'll just have to give hit some time. Ain't got no deadline no ways," said Omie.

"Ma, you and Pa a'gonna set up all night and jaw? I'm a'getting weary. I'm a'going to bed," Amie said.

"Amie, you water them pore chickens? If not, do hit 'fore you go to bed; you hear?"

"Yes, Sir, Pa. I done done it."

"Omie, I reckon I'm about done in too. You ready?"

"Yeah, March, let me put some 'taters in the ashes, and I'll be ready."

March was up early and went to the creek to see if it had gone down any. He was unable to detect any change from last evening. As he turned to go he saw a big soft-shell turtle in the shallow water near the road. March made a lunge and managed to catch him. He couldn't help saying out loud to himself, "Now, there's some mighty fine eating. Omie will be proud to get him, I bet."

When March got back, Omie was up and cooking flapjacks. Amie was turning logs, looking for beetles and worms for the chickens. March turned the turtle on his back to keep him from crawling off until he could butcher him. "Hey, look what I got fer yore dinner," he cried.

Omie looked and said, "That'll make some mighty fine stew. You ready fer some of these here 'jacks?"

"Yep, I shore am. How about you, Amie?"

"I'm ready, Pa. I wish we could turn these poor chickens out and let them scratch fer theirselves. Why don't we just eat them, Pa? They ain't a'laying any eggs no how."

"I 'spect there will come a time when we'll be glad to do just that," March replied. "We been lucky so far. Omie, after I eat, I'm going to see if I can kill us a deer. That shore was good stew that Jack fixed, and I aim to have me some more."

Omie said, "Clean that turtle 'fore you go, and I'll put it to stewing. Maybe we'll fry some of it fer supper, too. Keep yore eyes open fer some wild onions while yore out. We ain't got but one or two onions left. Food shore ain't much good without a passel of 'em."

The turtle cleaned, March cut more firewood until he was satisfied Omie had enough for the day. He went to the creek for a fresh bucket of water, then shouldered his gun and left, promising to return before dark.

He followed the edge of the water as he carefully made his way. Several times he came upon a moccasin stretched out on a log, or in a sunny spot along the edge of the water. March thought out loud, "I 'spect all this water is full of snakes. I best be careful. Shore don't need to be snake bit." Once, he saw a big alligator lying in the sun. He thought to himself, "Old boy, if'n I weren't a'looking fer a deer, I would be a'eating 'gator tail fer shore tomorrow." He saw several 'coons and lots of squirrels, but not a sign of a deer. Once, he heard a turkey gobble in the distance.

There was lots of water everywhere. March walked on, trying to stay on dry land as much as possible. He had been walking steadily for about two hours without success. Weary he sat down with his back against a big hickory tree hoping something would come along for him to shoot. It was warm and March felt drowsy. Soon he was fast asleep.

Quite a bit of time passed. March woke up suddenly. Something was coming his way. He sat perfectly still -- moving only his eyes, trying to see what was coming. Suddenly, not more than fifty feet away a wild hog came into view. He was rooting among the leaves and chewing something.

March eased his gun to his shoulder. He aimed just in front of the hog's shoulder and squeezed the trigger. When the bullet hit the hog, he sat down on his haunches as if to rest, then rolled over without a quiver.

March sat still for a while to see if there were other hogs with him. He knew that wild hogs can be very protective of one another and with their long tushes, very dangerous.

He stood and slowly approached his kill. Seeing no sign of life in him, March knelt and plunged his knife into the hog's heart to let the blood drain away. March spoke out loud to himself, "I'm glad I got a hog rather than a deer. Ain't nothing I'd ruther have than a bunch of fresh fried pork chops, unless hit's a big old pot of ribs and rice. We can render what's left into lard. Lord knows we need all the lard we can get. Have some cracklings fer pone, too. Boy, I could eat two, three hoecakes right now."

He deftly gutted the hog and cut off the head. No sense packing any more than necessary. Luckily, the hog wasn't full grown. March was able to get him on his shoulder and start for camp. He decided to leave the water and headed for dry ground, where the walking would be easier.

"I ought to be getting close to camp by now," March surmised as the last light of day faded away. He hollered several times, thinking Omie would hear him.

When he got no answer, he continued on. Suddenly he was walking in water again. Several times he stepped into deep holes almost over his head. He searched for dry land but couldn't find it.

He began to worry, talking out loud for comfort, "What if I'm lost and cain't get out of this water? Where will I spend the night? I cain't stand up all night."

He stood still listening, trying to decide which way camp lay. He hollered again and again, hoping Omie would hear and answer him. He shifted his burden and moved on.

He wondered what Omie and Amie were thinking about now. They must be worried. Thank goodness, it wasn't dark nights. The moon was just beginning to rise. There would be some light. He slogged on, his burden growing heavier with each step.

Several times he thought about just throwing the hog away, but he knew how much they needed the meat, especially the lard. He staggered on.

There was a violent crash of water just in front of him. A huge 'gator rushed away. March's heart nearly stopped beating. He had to hang on to a tree for support until his knees quit shaking.

March decided he would fire his gun in the hopes that Omie would hear it and answer. He fired and was reloading, when he heard in the distance the sound of metal on metal.

Thank God, Omie and Amie heard him. They were beating on the frying pan. March finished reloading and fired again. Back came the reassuring ring of the frying pan. He hurried on as fast as he could through waist deep water.

They continued to beat the pan, directing him to safety. Soon he could hear their voices shouting for him, and he answered back. They were waiting for him at the water's edge. March stumbled on to dry land with a hoarse whisper of, "Thank God, that's over."

Omie said, "We shore got worried when you didn't get back at dark. Amie wanted to come a'looking fer you. What happened? You get losted?"

March replied, "Let's get to camp, and I'll tell y'all about it."

He was exhausted, but as he told his story he regained his strength. "I thought fer shore an old 'gator was a'going to have hisself a right nice snack in the middle of whatever I was in. I ain't never been more scared than when that old 'gator flounced and flung water all over me. Lordy, Lordy, but I'm glad to be out of that. Got us a hog though. Pork chops fer breakfast?"

"All you want and a big pot of spareribs and rice fer dinner. When we gets them cracklings, we're going to have all the crackling bread we want too."

"I better skin that hog 'fore I go to bed and hang him up so's you can cook some of it fer breakfast."

"Hang him high, so's no varmints can get at him."

By the light of the fire, March skinned the shoat quickly and hung it up. Omie and Amie were ready for bed so they all turned in for a good night's rest.

Chapter 5

When March awoke, the sun was just peeking over the pine tops. He heard Omie making breakfast. She had flour bread, pork chops, grits, and hot sassafras tea ready when he came to the fire.

"How come you to get up so early, Omie?"

"We got to render that hog. You want some crackling bread, don't ye? Hit'll take most of the day, I 'spect."

As soon as breakfast was over, March filled the washpot with pork to be rendered and started it cooking. By mid-afternoon they had finished. They had a half-can of lard and lots of cracklings. If they used the cracklings in the bread Omie made each day, they would be used up before they turned rancid. The lard would keep for a much longer time, but that wasn't a problem. They used a large amount each day making bread and for all the frying that was done. Some would be used to grease the wagon wheels and some applied to their shoes to soften and waterproof them.

Next morning Omie rose at daylight, cooked a pot of grits and fried more pork chops. After breakfast she announced to March, "Me and Amie got to wash clothes today. I want you to carry the washpot down to the creek, fill it with water, and get a fire started to boil these dirty clothes. I cooked a'plenty to last all day, but you can put on a pot of ribs to boil and add some rice when they's about done."

"All right. I guess I'll cut some more firewood too. No telling how long we's got to stay here."

After Omie and Amie had hung the washed clothes to dry, back at camp they found March lying under a tree with his mouth wide open, fast asleep. Scattered all around were the chickens, each with a string tied to its foot and fastened to a tree. They were scratching for all they were worth, searching for grubs and worms. March had a huge pile of firewood cut and stacked nearby. Omie whispered to Amie, "Well, he might as well rest up. That old creek is still a'roaring."

It was three days more before March judged it safe to cross. It was good to be on their way again. Even the mules seemed to be glad to leave.

Once across the creek, the elevation of the land rose and the water disappeared. They were making pretty good time. March estimated they had come about twelve miles since crossing the creek.

Rounding a bend in the road, they could see a house and barn beside the road. In the yard several children were playing in the dirt.

When the children heard the creak of the wagon they all stood and gazed with wide eyes at what they must surely have thought was an apparition. One child ran behind the house.

A man and woman appeared. They all stood looking until March stopped the wagon. The man spoke out, "You folks get down and rest a spell and water yore stock. Where you folks a'going to?"

March answered, "I reckon we're headed for Valdosta. Is this the right way?"

"I ain't never been myself. I reckon you can get there from here. You folks get down and set a spell with us. We be the Parnells. I'm Will; my woman there, Bessie. We don't get a right smart of visitors out here. It gets mighty lonesome fer the wife and kids." March could tell they were starved for company and news from the outside world.

Will helped March unhitch the wagon and water the stock. Omie and Amie sat down on the edge of the porch with Bessie and the children to talk. When March and Will joined them, Will said, "It's getting on near to supper time. We ain't got much, but you and your family are shore welcome to what we's got. Ain't no use you folks traveling on, seeing how the day's mostly gone anyhow. You all jes' stay right here with us fer the night."
Omie and Amie were starved for company. Omie said quickly to March, "Let's do hit. I'm tired of listening to crickets and frogs. I want to talk some."
March replied, "Well if they can put up with us, I shore don't mind."

The women folks cooked and talked, and Omie shared her snuff. "I ain't had a good dip of snuff fer a spell," Bessie said. "We don't hardly ever leave this place. Ain't got no reason to neither. We's just getting by out here. We live mostly from what we gets out of the woods, a'hunting and a'fishing mostly. 'Course, we have a little garden too, but hit's a job a'keeping the varmints from a'eating hit up."

They talked until late evening before finally wearing out what news each had for the other. They all turned in for a few hours of rest.

March had the team hitched and ready at sun-up. Before leaving Will gave them directions to the next town. Omie shared some more of her snuff and traded some lard for sweet potatoes. As they pulled out, they said their good-byes. They felt as though they were leaving family. The Parnells waved to them as they drove away.

For the next few days the little McCloud family rolled from one crossroads to another. The country was sparsely settled. Houses were few and far between.

As they traveled, they supplemented their diet with gophers, turtles and fish caught from the numerous ponds and creeks. Berries of all kinds were just beginning to ripen. Mother Nature's larder was filled, and her store was open with no charge!

The land here was different from South Carolina's. It was low and flat, covered with thick undergrowth and filled with lakes and streams.

Gradually, as they traveled to the southwest, the land became more settled. Houses and farms were seen more often. People were curious about them. They wanted to know where they were going, and where they had come from. They wanted to hear about their adventures along the roads.

Whenever they encountered people, March was sure to inquire about job opportunities. From time to time, he was able to hire out the team for a day or two of plowing. He would gladly do any job that would bring a few coins for expenses. Most of the time he had to take his pay in produce or some other goods, but those were things they would have to buy anyway. Tough times weren't limited to Carolina. They were everywhere.

They had been on the road for more than a month. As near as March could tell, they were not even halfway to their destination. Living out of a wagon and sleeping on the ground were getting tiresome.

Cooking and washing clothes were doubly hard for the women. Bending over wash tubs placed on the ground was a back breaker. Their clotheslines were bushes and available limbs.

When Omie compared it to living back in South Carolina, though, she admitted it wasn't too different after all. So far they had done very well, considering everything. They still had most of the three dollars they started out with and plenty of food. She admitted it was exciting seeing other places and meeting different people.

One grueling day a wheel on the wagon dropped into a hole. The mules bolted. The shift was too much for the wagon tongue to take, and it broke. They unloaded the wagon and made camp.

March selected a hickory tree to use to make the new tongue. He spent the better part of one whole day with his ax working it into the proper shape.

He needed a brace and bit to make new bolt holes, but he didn't have one. He would have to try and find one. They had passed a house several miles back. Maybe he could borrow one there.

Early the next morning, March set out riding one of the mules in his search for a bit. He found the house they had passed, but the man only had a very small bit. It would have to do. March promised to return the tool as soon as possible and hurried back to camp. He arrived just as darkness fell. The repairs would have to wait for morning.

After breakfast, March started work on the tongue. When he finished boring the holes, he heated an iron rod to the red hot point, then drove it into the existing holes. It burned and charred the inside of the hole. When it cooled, he hammered it out and did it all over again. It took a long time, but finally March succeeded in enlarging the hole sufficiently for the bolts to fit. He drove in the bolts, and the tongue was secured to the wagon.

It was late that afternoon when March returned the borrowed tool. In the three full days March had spent working on the wagon tongue, Omie and Amie hunted berries and made scrumptious pies. They also found a pond full of fish that were anxious to grace their table.

It was good to be back on the road. Even the mules stood still for March to harness them. At all times angling south by southwest, they marched steadily to make up the lost time.

They passed through a host of small villages, places that were mostly names: Carterville, Clovis Corners, Mulberry, Saps Mill, Poker Town, Newly, Limestone, Sparta and a dozen more. At every farm or village March sought work. It was the same story everywhere, "Ain't no work here-bouts, Mister. Couldn't pay you no how."

Most farms were small, just five or ten acres. One man could handle the work alone.

Whenever there was work, March stopped long enough to do it. Once, they stayed for a week. March earned three dollars. Of course, he supplied the mules and plow, along with his labor. He was proud of that three dollars. "Omie, soon as we get to a store," he said "I'm a'going to buy us a little coffee and some white sugar to put in hit. I ain't had no coffee in so long, I'm beginning to dream about hit. I'm a'gonna get me some Bull Durham smoking tobacco too. Y'all can get you some more snuff."

True to his word, at the very next store March bought two pounds of Arbuckle coffee and a sack of Bull Durham smoking tobacco. Amie and Omie each got a box of snuff.

They could hardly wait until the next meal, so they could have some coffee. Knowing it would be a long time before they got any more, they boiled the coffee grounds over and over, until every drop of goodness was extracted from them. March even tried smoking the grounds after they were dry by adding a little Bull Durham, but he gave up saying, "I cain't smoke these things. I ain't a'getting nothing but fire."

Day followed weary day as they moved on. One day March discovered the iron tires were coming off the rims. They made camp next to a creek. March jacked the wagon up and removed the wheels. He laid them in the creek to soak. He let them stay for a night and a day, until the wood swelled and tightened the tires.

The animals had a good rest and enjoyed good grazing. Omie did a lot of special cooking with the extra time on her hands.

March caught a mess of bullfrogs from the creek, while Amie held the fire so he could see their eyes. Next morning before leaving, they dined on frog legs. "Ain't nothing gooder than fried frog legs, lessen hit's fried chicken," March opined.

As they moved on, they passed through the biggest town since Savannah, named Waycross, Georgia. After that came Coffeeville, Alamander, Soda Springs, Niceville, Dorcas, Needmore, Plenty, Paynes Crossroads, Zoar and a host more, all of them more name than substance.

Once more the land became flat. It was filled with low ponds and palmetto, wiregrass, and pine trees. The pines made the temperature soar. The palmettos were filled with "seed ticks" and "red bugs" so tiny that they were almost invisible. Exasperated, Omie said, "When them little old red bugs bite, they itch so bad, you can't stop a'scratching until the blood runs." They all looked like they had been shot with a scatter gun from the many bites.

Chapter 6

One day after making camp, Omie and Amie got their buckets and went to pick gooseberries for pies. While they were picking, Omie, so intent on the job at hand, failed to see a huge rattlesnake under the bushes. The snake struck her on the calf of her leg. It felt like a red hot needle had been stuck into her leg. The pain was intense. She yelled for Amie, "Come and help me, I's been struck by a rattler."

Amie threw down her bucket and came running. Omie warned her away from the buzzing reptile, "Look out Amie, he's under that berry bush; he's a big 'un!"

Amie helped Omie back to camp. By the time they arrived, Omie's leg was swollen nearly twice the size of the other one. She was screaming so loud, March was scared half to death.

Excitedly, Omie told him what happened. March said, "Quick, Amie, put that rope around yore Ma's leg just above where the snake struck her. Now, draw it tight. Omie, this here is a'gonna hurt some, but we's got to get that pizen drawed out." He made a cross-cut over the fang marks, then began sucking the blood and poison out, spitting it on the ground. Then he loosened the rope to let more blood flow in. He repeated the procedure several times.

By nightfall, Omie's leg had swollen so large the skin began to split apart. Her temperature soared, and March said to Amie, "Yore Ma is so sick; she's going out of her head."

"Is Ma a'going to die, Pa?"

"I don't know, Amie, I've done all I know how to do. I reckon hit's up to God, now."

"Do you reckon God will cure her, Pa?"

"I jus' don't know, honey."

March sat up all night putting cold rags on Omie's forehead, trying to cool her fever. She was in and out of her senses. It was all March could do to restrain her. Amie cooked breakfast and relieved March so he could get some rest.

When March got up at noon Omie wasn't any better. Her leg was bluish-black and swollen so big that it looked like it belonged to something other than a human. Her fever was still raging. With every breath, she cried out with pain.

Amie asked, "Pa, what we a'gonna do; cain't we take her to a doctor?"

"No, honey, there ain't no doctor that I know of. I don't even know if there's anybody close to us. We'll just have to do the best we can by ourselves."

"I shore am scared Ma's a'going to die, Pa."

"Amie, I'm a'gonna take one of the mules and ride a ways to see if I can find anybody that might help us. I'll go a few miles, and if I don't see somebody I'll come on back 'fore dark. You stay with your Ma and keep them cold rags on her to keep the fever down. Try to get a little water down her, too, if you can."

"All right, Pa. Hurry back as fast as you can."

March rode away on one of the mules at a gallop, soon disappearing from Amie's sight. He rode several miles without seeing anyone or any sign that anyone had passed recently. Though he hated to turn back, he must return before dark or run the risk of getting lost himself.

He hurried back as fast as the mule would go. When he came to the camp there was an Indian sitting next to a tree. The first thought that ran through March's head was, "Indians have killed my family!" March got down from the mule expecting to be attacked, but the Indian continued to sit and stare at him.

Just then Amie appeared and shouted, "Oh, Pa, I'm glad yore back, but Ma ain't no better. I been a'keeping cold rags on her like you told me to, but her fever ain't broke yet. Did you find any help?"

"No, I ain't seen anybody. Amie, who's this here Indian, and where did he come from?"

"I don't know where he came from, Pa. He just suddenly appeared. Liked to have scared the daylights out of me. I thought fer shore I were a goner and Ma too. But, Pa, he's all right, and he can talk American too. I told him about Ma, and he said he would make medicine for her; so I let him."

"What kind of medicine did he make?"

"I don't know, Pa. He went down to the creek and caught a big old bullfrog and split him open and put hit over the place where the snake bit Ma. Then he went out to that patch of palmetto and pulled some of them berries off and boiled them. Then he made Ma drink a cup of the juice."

March turned to the Indian and said, "My little girl says you talk American. My name is March. March McCloud. What did you give to my wife? Will hit make her well?"

"We not know if she get well; maybe two days. This Indian medicine. All Indians know this medicine, use when snake bites. Sometime work, sometime not work. Have to wait and see."

"What's yore name?" March asked.

"White man call me "Sumbitch." I called Hawk by my people."

"Well, Hawk, I want to thank you fer what you are trying to do. Are there any more with you?"

"No, I only one left; all others go away with "soljers" or run away and hide. I hide in woods; no come out; no let people see me."

"Hawk, why did you come out and let us see you?"

"I watch you. You not "soljer." You treat womans good. You treat mules good. I think you good man. Not try to make Hawk leave place where I always live. I see what trouble you have. I try to help, if you want."

"You are right, Hawk; I ain't interested in making you or anybody else go anywhere. You are welcome at our camp. Thank you fer your help."

March staked the mule and went to Omie. He felt her forehead. She was still burning up with fever. Other than bathing her face with cool water, he could only stand and watch her suffer.

Along toward dark Amie called him to come and eat. Hawk was still sitting by the tree. He arose when March called to him, "Come and eat with us, Hawk; we got plenty fer us all. You are more than welcome."

"I eat only if Hawk bring meat for you to cook."

"Come on then. When we finish eating we'll talk."

When they had finished eating, March rolled a cigarette and gave it to Hawk and then rolled one for himself. He picked up a burning stick from the fire and lighted their cigarettes. They smoked for a while, not talking, just thinking their private thoughts. Finally March began to tell Hawk where they had come from and where they were going. He told Hawk of the things that had happened to them on their trip.

Then Hawk spoke, "I born here, this place; plenty long time ago. My father born here. Him father born here. It has always been so. Until the white man come, we only have other Indians to make war with. We kill many of them; they kill many my people. It has always been so. We have plenty animals to eat, make clothes. We make houses from little pine tree. Cover with palmetto to keep out rain, cold wind. We never sick. Snake make us sick when bite. Plenty fish, plenty 'gator for to eat. Eat top of palmetto tree, plenty good. All very good till white man come. Tell us leave his land. Not white men's land. Great Spirit give us this land when Great Spirit make world. Now, white man say this not our land no more. Tell me why this is? Why white men say now this their land? Never see white men since Great Spirit make world. Now he say land his. How this be?"

"Hawk, the white man is new to this country. Yore right, the land was yours until you gave us the right to live on hit. Now there are more and more white people. We are used to owning the land where we come from. It ain't right fer the white man to take the land and forbid the Indian to live on hit anymore. Hawk, I don't make the laws. Others do that. I got to do what somebody tells me to do, same as you do. I'm free to go where I want to, but I cain't call the land mine unless I pay fer it. I wish I could explain hit to you. I don't understand why hit's this a'way. I know in my heart hit's wrong; I'm sorry. I shore hope you don't hate me."

"I feel my heart you not want to kill Indian. You and me will be friend. Now we give your squaw medicine."

On the third day after Omie was bitten, she began to show some improvement. Hawk replaced the frog on Omie's leg two times every day. At first the frog turned green as it drew the poison from Omie's leg. Then as the poison lessened, the frog was less green. Hawk said it was a sign the poison was leaving.

On the fourth day Omie opened her eyes and recognized March and Amie. Her temperature began to drop. Next day she was able to eat some turtle soup Amie made for her. Her leg remained swollen, black from thigh to the bottom of her foot. Where her skin had broken open, it scabbed over and began to itch, a sure sign of healing. When she saw Hawk for the first time she screamed. She, too, thought he was going to murder her. But Amie came running to see what was the matter, and she assured Omie that all was well. She explained to Omie that Hawk had saved her life. In a few days Omie was able to walk with the help of a crutch March made for her. After that she made a rapid recovery.

Hawk stayed at the camp, leaving only to hunt. He brought in a deer, some pumpkins and squash. He taught them how to harvest the white meat from the tops of the cabbage palm. He showed March how to make an Indian house from little trees and how to cover them with palmetto leaves to keep out the rain and wind, and always he continued to make medicine for Omie. He and Omie had long talks. Like March, Omie tried as best she could to explain the white man's way. Hawk would just look at her and say, "I not understand white men. They want Indian land. Then sell; go away." Omie had no words of comfort for the one who had saved her life.

They stayed here until Omie was able to drive the wagon. Then one morning they loaded up and were ready to resume their journey. As March hitched the team, Omie and Amie said their good-byes to Hawk. Omie said to him, "Hawk, we wish you could come with us, but hit's against the white man's law. We'll never ferget you. I wish there was some way I could repay you fer saving my life."
"Hawk have no need for pay. Hawk do for anyone. You now my friend. If you come again this place, you make camp, same place. Hawk will come, find you, if Great Spirit not come for me. You not tell others Hawk live this place."
They drove away, tears moistening their eyes. No better friend in all the world could they have found than Hawk. Not once did he ever ask for anything. True to his promise, he hunted and supplied meat and vegetables in exchange for the food he ate. March gave Hawk all the tobacco he had and one of his knives as a token of their friendship.

Chapter 7

The land they journeyed through now was sparsely settled with distances greater between settlements. Sometimes three or four days would pass without coming into contact with anyone. They continued living off the land, catching gophers, turtles and fish in abundance. The lessons learned from Hawk served them well, especially harvesting the palmetto cabbage. They learned to cook it by adding some side meat. It was delicious. It provided the starch they needed in their diet.

When they stopped for more than a day, March quickly built a palmetto shelter for Omie to cook in if the weather was bad. They fell into the rhythm of the road once more, and life was fine.

From the next person they met they made a startling discovery. They had passed far to the south of their intended destination of Valdosta. Unbelieving, March said, "I cain't believe we got so fer off the track. I thought we followed directions purty good, but I reckon we missed the mark som'mers." March questioned the man closely for some time. He asked about the farming in the area. "What about the possibility of a job?" He got the same answer he had gotten from others along their route. There were no jobs; farms were poor and small.

March continued questioning the man, "We heard there was good farming around Valdosta; that's where we were headed. Do you know if that's true?"

"Yeah, I heered that too. I reckon the farming is good enough, but they's a sight of people there; more'n can get work. Ain't no good houses to stay in neither. I heered from a feller t'other day there were fine farm land and some work to be had around Monticello or Tallahassee. That's over in Floridee; a right smart way off."

March asked for directions to get there; then he thanked him and turned to Omie and said, "You heered what he said, sounds like we're closer to Monticello than Valdosta. Reckon we ought to just go on the way we're headed?"

Omie answered, "I don't reckon hit matters; we don't know nothing fer sure about either place." They decided on the spot to keep going toward Monticello. They had been traveling now for almost three months. It seemed like forever, and some of the things that had happened to them along the way were hard to believe. They had forded countless creeks and rivers and passed by or through dozens of places. Some had names, most did not. They encountered few people along the way who didn't stand out in their minds for one reason or another.

Soon they learned they were in Florida. Several days later they entered the little town of Madison. After that the villages of Greenville, Aucilla, Lamont, Capps, and finally into Monticello.

Monticello was a bustling village of a hundred or more people. They made their camp along a pretty creek not far from town.

The next day March started his search for a job although he knew all the crops had been planted and much of the work was finished. With his mules and wagon he hoped to help with the harvest. He followed up on every lead he heard about, but for one reason or the other, he failed to obtain work.

When they arrived in Monticello, they still had the last three dollars March had earned and five cents of the original three dollars they had before leaving Pine Top. They were still able to live off the land, but that wasn't enough. What they needed was a house to live in and a steady job.

March didn't want to remain a sharecropper working for someone else, but without land or funds what could he do? He couldn't borrow from a bank; he wasn't known, nor had he any collateral. Omie and Amie stood by him with encouragement every day. "You'll shorely get something soon," they kept saying to him. But days passed without prospects; they were down to a few coins, and the staple goods were dwindling, and their clothing was wearing out. Maybe, if he went to Tallahassee he might find something there. March made a decision. Next week, if he was still without a job, he would go there.

A few days later March stopped in the livery stable to hear the gossip. While he was talking to the owner, a prosperous looking man came in. He stood and listened to March vent his woes on the owner of the livery stable for a while, then he said to the owner. "I'm Mr. Price. I think you know who I am. I am the owner of El Destino Plantation. I wish to rent a horse to go there. I will send one of the slaves back with the horse tomorrow." Then turning to March he said, "My good man, I heard what you said about being out of work. What can you do? Do you know cotton? Can you plant and supervise a farm?"

March was so startled by his rapid questions that he was almost tongue tied. "Yes, Sir, to all of yore questions. I've farmed cotton all my life in South Caroline. If the land hadn't wore out I'd still be there. Sir, if yore land is any good, I can raise you as good a crop of cotton as can be had."

"Fine, fine, I will be at El Destino Plantation for the next few days. Come see me tomorrow. Can I count on you?"

"Yes, Sir, my word is my bond. Would noon time be suitable?"

"Noon time tomorrow will be just fine."

He gave March directions to El Destino Plantation, then returned to his business of renting a horse. Soon he mounted and rode away. March turned to the owner of the stables and questioned him about Mr. Price.

The owner of the stables let him know right away he was dealing with a very rich man who owned not only El Destino Plantation but also Chemonie Plantation near Miccosukee, and another in Georgia. More than two hundred slaves were required to tend them. "I just heered t'other day his overseer got drunk, and a hoss throwed him and broke his neck. I reckon that's what old man Price wants you fer. If you suit him and get the job, you'll be fixed."

"Well, I shore hope I suit him then."

Chapter 8

March hurried back to camp. He related his encounter with Mr. Price to Amie and Omie. They were excited and wanted to know everything that transpired between them.

March answered their questions as best he could. They sat quietly contemplating what it might mean to them. Omie said, "March, I shore do hope you get that job. I hope there's a nice little house fer us to live in, and most of all I hope he pays you good money."

Not to be left out Amie said, "Pa, I hope they's some horses I can ride, and I hope there's somebody my age fer me to have fer company."

They talked on until dark about their hopes and dreams for the future.

Finally March said, "We better get to bed early. I've got to be there at twelve o'clock tomorrow. I sure as heck cain't afford to be late." Everyone agreed that would be a sure way to lose a job. They went to bed, their heads spinning with fantasies.

At first light, March was up making ready to go. While Omie made breakfast, March selected one of the mules he would ride. He curried him and fussed over his mane and tail making sure he looked its best.

After breakfast, he mounted and said, "Wish me luck."

"Good luck. Hope you get the job!" shouted Amie.

"We'll be waiting fer you. Hurry back!" cried Omie.

"I will. Don't you worry. Come up, mule. Let's go get that job!"

March thought it would take him about three hours to ride the fifteen miles to El Destino. If he arrived early, he would stop somewhere and wait. He wanted to arrive at the promised time, exactly twelve o'clock.

March did get there just a little early. He stopped and rested the mule and wiped the sweat from him. When he rode up to the house, it was exactly twelve o'clock. Mr. Price was sitting on the porch when March rode up. He called out, "Get down, McCloud, come in and sit down. I like a man who is prompt; shows he means business. McCloud, Martha, my cook, has prepared some lunch. Come eat with me and we'll discuss the job."

"That will be fine, Sir, I'm much obliged fer yore hospitality."

Just then Martha came to the door. She announced dinner was being served. "We'll be right there as soon as we wash our hands. Come on, McCloud, we have soap and water on the back porch."

After washing up they went into the house, and March saw the largest dining table he had ever seen. "I bet it would seat twenty or thirty people," he thought to himself. And the size of the dining room was unbelievable. March had never seen such a huge room just for eating in. He felt ill at ease.

"Sit down, sit down. Martha will serve us. We don't eat a large lunch. We take our main meal in the evening," Mr. Price said.

The only thing March could think to say was, "Yes, Sir."

Martha brought fried chicken, biscuits, and mashed potatoes with gravy. Next she returned with large bowls of snap beans, squash and okra. March had never seen so much food for two people. "If his main meal is at night, I wonder what he eats then," he thought.

Martha came back in with a pitcher of buttermilk and placed it on the table. Mr. Price said, "Help yourself to a glass of buttermilk. It goes mighty well with this little lunch."

Again, all March could think to say was, "Yes, Sir; thank you, Sir."

When they finished Martha brought them each a large bowl of peach cobbler hot from the oven. She placed one before March, and the other she gave to Mr. Price saying, "I sho hopes yo'all likes dis heah cobbler. I picked the peaches dis mawning, and it am hot from de oven."

"Martha, I didn't see any peaches around here. I bet those peaches came from a can," Mr. Price said, with a wink to March.

"Na, Suh, Marser Price, dey sho nuf come from dem trees out behind the hoss lot. You members dem, don'cha, Marser Price?"

"Now that you mention it, I do seem to remember seeing some peach trees somewhere, Martha."

"Marser Price, you is funning me now."

When they finished eating the cobbler, Martha brought each of them a hot cup of coffee. March thought to himself so vividly, he wondered if maybe he said the words out loud, "Man, this is high living. I shore do wish that Omie and Amie could be here with me a'setting at this big old table a'eating all this here fancy food."

Next, March was offered a cigar, but he declined thinking to himself, "If I set here and smoke a cigar with this highfalutin big shot, why, I'd look like a fool."

Mr. Price said as he stood, "Come along, McCloud. Let's go sit on the porch. Are you ready to discuss business?"

"Yes, Sir, Mr. Price. I'm ready."

March followed him to the porch. Mr. Price said, "Take that rocker, McCloud, and make your self comfortable. Tell me all about yourself. Where do you come from? What's been your farming experience, and how did you come to be in Monticello?"

March started at the beginning. He told Mr. Price of his childhood back in Pine Top, South Carolina, and about his parents. He related how the land had been overworked, bringing about the steady decline of the cotton crop and described the measures he and his father had taken trying to improve the yields.

Mr. Price mostly sat and grunted. Occasionally he asked for specific details about certain things. March responded the best he knew how. Mr. Price seemed not to be too concerned with what March was saying, but March could see in his eyes that he was paying close attention. He sensed that Mr. Price was well acquainted with farming and the mechanics of it too.

When March finished, Mr. Price said, "McCloud, I have listened to you very carefully. I believe you are a truthful man. I also believe that you are a pretty good farmer. Now, let me tell you a little about myself."

Mr. Price touched briefly on his childhood, but quickly came to the more recent portion of his life. He spent the better part of his time in New York City. He told March his major interests were located there.

---And so---the man who ran this plantation would be on his own. He would have to work independently and make day-to-day decisions that might affect not only the financial integrity of El Destino, but also the lives of the slaves who worked the land. He let March know that whoever might be the overseer would have to be aggressive and seize control at once. By that he meant the boss had to act like a boss and not be overly friendly with the workers.

He named each of his fields and what was planted in them, quoting yields for the last several years. He named the slaves and what they did best, singling out the ones who were in a position of authority, such as Martha, who was in charge of the kitchen. He emphasized that position was only when he and his family were in residence at El Destino. There would be no unannounced visitors. If anyone showed up without an authorization letter signed by Mr. Price they would not be allowed to stay. "Can you enforce that order, Mr. McCloud?"

"I'll carry out your orders to the letter, Sir."

He told March about the boy who was responsible for the stables, the blacksmith, the gang leaders, and what their positions entitled them to. Finally, Mr. Price told him about George who was over the others.

"George can't read or write, but he knows what grows best where and when it's time to plant. He also keeps the rest of the people in line. If there is a discipline problem, and there will be, George should be notified. Let him handle it if possible. You will have to be the judge of that. George is subject at all times to you, but I have found in dealing with a large group of people that it is best to delegate a little authority, if you know what I mean. It makes others feel as if they are having a say about the running of things. They will be more content. Another thing, Mr. McCloud, if a worker becomes sick and in your judgment he needs to see a doctor, then Doc Riley will come if necessary. If the worker is well enough to go see the doctor, then they will go to him. Now then, Mr. McCloud, after hearing all this are you still interested in the position of overseer of El Destino?"

March had been paying close attention as Mr. Price talked and without hesitation answered, "Yes, Sir, Mr. Price, I shorely am."

"McCloud, let me tell you how I came to need an overseer at this particular time. Three days ago word came to me at my Georgia plantation near Albany that the overseer here had an accident and was dead. I'm told he was drunk and attempted to ride an unbroken horse. The horse threw him. When he hit the ground his neck was broken. As far as I'm concerned, he got what he deserved. He had no business riding a horse while drinking. Furthermore, if I had known he was a "drinker," as he apparently was, then I would have replaced him at once. Mr. McCloud, are you a drinker?"

"Mr. Price, I'd be a liar if I said I never take a drink. On occasion I do take a drink, but just to be sociable. I've got a wife and daughter I'm responsible fer. My first obligation is fer their welfare. To answer your question, no, Sir, I ain't a drinker."

"Mr. McCloud, it hadn't crossed my mind that you might have a family. In the past I have only hired single men. We are somewhat isolated here, and your wife won't have any company to speak of. As for your children, there is no school close by. I know that some think book-learning is unnecessary. I am not one of those. Mr. McCloud, if I hire you how will you handle that problem?"

"Well, Sir, first off let me say I agree with you. I want my daughter to have as much schooling as we can give her. We've looked into the possibility of sending her to a boarding school in Monticello when I find work, and we can afford it."

"That's commendable, McCloud, but can you afford the cost?" Mr. Price asked.

March asked, "What will this job pay?"

"The job pays two hundred a year, paid at the completion of the year."

March was afraid to ask if he had heard right, two hundred dollars a year! "Well, Sir, I want to be truthful with you. Right now I ain't got no savings and no way to borrow none neither. I got two fine mules; that's one of them I rode here today. The other one is identical to this one. I believe I can sell them and my wagon and plows fer enough to get by on till I get paid."

"Mr. McCloud, it might be that I can use those mules and wagon and plows too. If I hire you, I will look at them and make you an offer. How does that sound to you?"

"That sounds most generous to me, Sir."

"Before we go any further, let me tell you some of the other things you can expect if you come to work here. First off, the house for the overseer isn't very large. It only has one bedroom. There is a shed room that could be pressed into service if necessary. There are no furnishings that come with it either. You are welcome to the contents that are in the house now. There would be no provisions allotted to your wife and child unless we make an adjustment in your salary, say to one hundred seventy-five dollars a year. Work pants and shoes will be provided for you, but there is nothing suitable for your wife and child. Can you handle that?"

"Yes, Sir, I can handle that."

"Good, good. Now let's go take a look at the house."

As Mr. Price had said, the house was not a mansion, but to March it certainly beat what he had. March said it would be suitable. Finally Mr. Price said, "Mr. McCloud, I'm between a rock and a hard place. I must be on my way to New York the first part of next week. I do not have another prospect to fill this job. If the conditions as I have described them to you are satisfactory and you can move your belongings in and be ready to take over Monday morning, the job is yours. What is your answer?"

"My answer, Sir, is I'll move in tomorrow. I'll be ready to take over first thing the next day. I thank you fer the opportunity."

"Good, good. Let's hope we'll have a prosperous arrangement for both of us. We will continue our discussion when you get moved in. I will fill you in with all the details you need to know."

"Then good day to you, Mr. Price. I'll be back tomorrow afternoon with my family."

"Oh, Mr. McCloud, there is one more thing. You can read and write, can't you? We'll need to correspond frequently."

"Yes, Sir, I do have some schooling, and though I don't get much practice, I think you'll be able to read and understand what I'll have to say."

"Fine, fine. Until tomorrow then. Good day to you, McCloud."

"Good day, Sir."

Chapter 9

At last a job! March was elated and could have floated home on one of the passing clouds. And the salary! March had to pinch himself! A hundred seventy-five dollars a year! It was a king's ransom. More than he'd ever dreamed of making. As March rode along, he dreamed of all the things they would be able to do with the money. "I wish Ma and Pa were still alive. I could help them a little," he thought.

When March rode into camp, Omie and Amie were waiting for him. Before he could get down from the mule, they wanted to know if he had gotten the job. When he said he had the job, they shrieked with joy. They hugged him and the three of them danced around together as soon as he got off the mule. "Before I answer any questions, let me tend to this mule. Is supper ready?"

"Supper's ready. Hurry along, we want to hear about everything that happened to you today!"

After March finished tending the mule and washed his hands, he filled his plate and sat down. Before he could take a bite of food, they both had questions for him.

He related the whole story starting with his trip to El Destino that morning. He told them what a large house

Mr. Price lived in and with unconcealed excitement he told them about eating dinner with Mr. Price in a dining room that was larger than any house they had ever lived in. And he told them about Martha and what a good cook she was. March related to them all that had transpired between him and Mr. Price, and finally how Mr. Price had offered him the job.

"Pa, how much pay you a'going to get?" Amie asked.

When March told them, they were speechless. The questions ceased, and they could only stare as they tried to calculate how much a hundred seventy-five dollars was.

March stood up and said, "We have to get up early tomorrow and break camp. I promised Mr. Price we would move in before the day is over. I shore intend to be there."

He also told them what Mr. Price had to say about schooling for Amie. March looked at Amie and said, "As soon as we can, Amie, we're a'going to enroll you in the girls' academy in Monticello. You'll be able to come home on the weekends. School is high on Mr. Price's list. We want you to have as much schooling as possible too. Mr. Price says they'll teach you all the social graces, too; whatever that is. Anyway there ain't but one bedroom. The house is kind of small. On the weekends, I'll sleep in the shed room. You and your Ma will have to sleep together. Besides, Mr. Price puts so much stock in school, that we cain't afford to rile him. He made an exception to his rule by hiring a family man."

"I ain't a'going to no school, Pa. I had enough already, I can read and write purty good."

"Now, Amie, they just ain't no use in a'talking about hit. That's just the way hit has to be, else I won't get the job. We cain't live here in the woods a'sleeping on the ground 'thout no money a'coming in."

Amie said, "I shore will be glad when I get rich; then I can do as I please. Pa, you won't have to work for nobody neither."

Omie said, "Hit won't be so bad, Amie. You'll get to be with other girls and larn all about everything. If you get some more book larning then maybe you won't have to live like we's been a'having to live. Besides, you'll be with us every Saturday and Sunday."

March said, "Ain't no use in jawing any more about hit tonight. We'll talk hit over some more tomorrow. Right now we better get to bed, we got a busy day ahead of us, and your Daddy's got to be right sharp so's he can hoss trade with Mr. Price."

They were up bright and early, eager to get started. After a hasty breakfast they broke camp. When they had the wagon loaded, they set out for El Destino full of hope and dreams for a better life. On the way they ate cold potatoes for their dinner and washed them down with water.

Along about two o'clock they came in sight of Mr. Price's big house. Omie and Amie couldn't believe how big it was. "My, my, wouldn't hit be something if we owned that house," Omie said.

Amie said, "One of these here days we's a'going to have one just like this'n; you just wait and see."

"I shore hope yore right, Amie girl, fer I can't hardly wait to set at that big old table and have me a servant gal to bring my food to me," said March.

Omie said, "Right now I'm satisfied to have a house of any kind."

March stopped the wagon in front of the little house that was to be their home and got down. Omie and Amie went inside and came right back out again.

"March McCloud, we ain't a'moving into that pig sty until we give hit a first class cleaning. It looks like the hogs have lived in hit and smells even worse," Omie said.

Amie agreed with her Ma and said, "Hit's even worse than camping out, Pa."

"I'll go see if I can find Mr. Price and tell him what we're a'fixing to do, but I don't reckon he'll care. While y'all are a'cleaning hit, don't ferget everything in there belongs to us," March said as he hurried away to find Mr. Price.

Omie and Amie began to empty the contents of the house into the yard. Omie said to Amie, "When March comes back tell him to unload that washpot and get hit to heating some water so's we can scrub this nasty place with some lye water. We need to chunk some boiling water on the walls to kill them chinches too."

"Yes'um, I'll go and look fer him."

"No, Amie. Better wait fer him to come back."

Soon, March came into view, and there was a man with him. They stopped and stood talking for a minute, then they came on to where Omie and Amie were.

"Howdy Ma'am, I'm Mr. Price--Dan Price--I want to welcome you and your daughter to El Destino. I hope you will be happy here. March informs me that you are less than pleased with the condition of the house. You are free to do with it as you like."

"Why, thank you, Mr. Price. When I get through with this place you won't know hit."

"Now, if you will excuse me, Ma'am, I have some things to attend to. March, if you will see me first thing in the morning we can get started. We have a lot of things to discuss before I leave."

"Yes, Sir, first thing in the morning, I'll be there."

Omie said to March, "Ferget putting a fire around the pot. Fer now we'll just take everything out, and Amie and me'll scrub tomorrow while you and Mr. Price talk."

Amie said, "I'll cook supper Ma. I reckon we plan on camping out like we been doing fer tonight."

"Yeah, them chinch bugs will eat us up in there."

They spent the remainder of the day getting everything out of the house and sorting through the clothes and bedding that had been left by the previous overseer.

The following day they were up early. After breakfast was over Omie wanted March to get a fire going around the washpot so she and Amie could start scrubbing the floors and walls. It would be an all day job. She warned March to be prepared for a skimpy dinner.

March was waiting by the porch when Mr. Price came down the steps. March greeted him with a hearty good morning. Mr. Price returned the greeting and said, "Well, are you ready to get started? We have a lot of ground to cover today."

"Yes, Sir, I'm ready if you are."

"Good, good. The first thing I'm going to do is to introduce you to George, then to the rest of the people. They are anxious to see and judge you."

"That's fine with me, Sir. Let's get started."

George was standing a short distance away as they spoke. Mr. Price motioned for him to come over. "George, this is Mr. McCloud. I have just hired him to be the new overseer. His wife and daughter will be living here as well. I'm sure you will continue to do the fine job for Mr. McCloud that you have always done."

"Yas, Suh, Mr. Price, I sho will," then turning to March he said, "I's glad to meet you, Suh."

"George, Mr. Price tells me you're a good farmer and know how to get things done. Fer now there won't be no changes as long as things run smoothly. You and I'll have to work closely 'til I learn my way around."

"Yas, Suh, Mr. McCloud, dat be fine."

Mr. Price broke in and dismissed George to his duties.

When he was gone Mr. Price said, "March, I liked the way you handled that. It shows George that you don't intend to show off your authority by telling him to be ready for changes. It tells him you will wait and evaluate what is presently being done. March, this plantation has about fifty-five hundred acres. I want to cover as much of it as we can today, so we'll ride horseback. Leroy is the stable boy. He has saddled the horses and is waiting for us. Come on."

When they got to the stables, Leroy was waiting by the doors with two beautiful horses. They climbed onto the horses and rode a short distance to the quarters where the slaves lived. George had them assembled, standing in a group. Leroy ran up and joined them. Mr. Price addressed them.

"This is Mr. McCloud. I have hired him to be the new overseer. You will treat him with respect. He is the boss. He is the only boss. What he says goes. George will continue just as he always has, and everyone else will continue in their same jobs for now. Mr. McCloud may want to make some changes in the future. If he does that's his business. We have a good crop in the ground, and it seems to be coming along just fine. You are all doing good work, and I want it to stay that way." Turning to March he asked, "I suppose you want to say a few words?"

"Yes, Sir, I reckon I do." Turning to face them he said, "I'll say the same thing to you that I said to George. Fer the time being, things will continue the same way they been a'going. When I learn my way around, I may want to do some things differently. I may, or may not want to farm a little different than what you are used to; that remains to be seen. I have been hired to make this plantation pay. I'll do my level best to do just that." With that he nodded to George signaling him to dismiss the hands. George told the slaves to head for the fields.

Mr. Price led the way as he and March rode over the property. He did most of the talking, pointing out things of interest as they rode. They visited each field under cultivation. He asked March to evaluate each one and paid close attention to his answers.

When dinner time came, Leroy came riding up with a basket of sandwiches made from biscuits stuffed with fried ham, and a jug of buttermilk. There were large pieces of peach pie for dessert.

After eating dinner they continued to ride and walk over the land. March was amazed at how large the plantation was. It would take a while to master it all.

The major crop was cotton. The next largest was corn. The corn would fatten the hogs and would be the main-stay of the slaves as well as March and his family. Corn was also used to feed the mules that were used to do the work on this huge place. Corn was needed to make grits and meal. Thousands of pounds would be required to sustain such a force--just how much March would learn later.

The sugar cane field consisted of about ten acres. After processing into syrup it would be used in cooking and baking. It sweetened most of the beverages drunk throughout the year. It was eaten at every meal, usually with cornbread or biscuits. Each family consumed vast amounts.

Three or four acres were planted with sweet potatoes, another staple a plantation couldn't do without. When sweet potatoes were dug they would be put into holes in the ground lined with pine straw. Then they would be sealed over with dirt, or banked. Sweet potatoes stored in this fashion would not freeze or rot for a long period of time.

Peanuts and chufa were grown mostly for the hogs. Some peanuts would be boiled while still green (fresh) and eaten by humans as a delicacy. When peanuts were dried they would be roasted (parched) and eaten. Peanut hay is rich in nutrition. It supplemented the fodder, the leaves harvested from the corn stalks after the corn is picked, in providing feed for the mules and horses.

There was a small patch of tobacco. It would be smoked in pipes or chewed. The plantation included fields of peas, beans, squashes, watermelons and pumpkins. Vast quantities would be canned for use during the winter. Of all the crops, the favorites of the slaves were watermelons and peanuts.

March was surprised at the immensity of it all. He wondered if he, after all his boasting, could measure up. He intended to give it his all. As they rode, he asked questions about past yields. Was Mr. Price satisfied with them? He inquired about weather patterns, and about the weevil, and if it had been a problem in Florida yet. They spent the entire day riding and evaluating the plantation.

It was almost dark when they returned. March was weary. He was not used to riding for extended periods of time, especially not on a lively horse. When they turned the horses over to Leroy, he and Mr. Price continued to talk. Mr. Price asked if he had any questions about what they had seen today. March wanted to know if the horses were a part of the plantation stock. If so, would he be free to ride them?

"Yes, yes, of course," Mr. Price replied. "You and your family may ride as much as you want to. These horses are blooded stock and very valuable. See that Leroy takes good care of them and exercises them daily."

"Mr. Price, I didn't mention we have a milk cow. If you don't want her here, I'll get rid of her."

"No, the cow will be all right. You can keep her in the pasture behind the stables along with the other cows. I keep two or three for making butter mostly. We like the buttermilk too, when we come for a visit. There's a bull; if your cow has a calf, you may sell it."

"That's most generous of you," March said.

"I don't know about you, but I'm about worn out. I will see you again in the morning, and we'll conclude our business." With that Mr. Price turned and walked toward the house.

When March came into the yard, Omie and Amie were just coming out of the house. They greeted March and asked how his day had been. He brought them up to date with all that had happened to him, including the dinner that was delivered by Leroy. Omie said they would not be able to sleep in the house tonight because it was still wet from the scrubbing they had given it. They had managed to find time to cook some supper, though, and as soon as March washed up they would eat.

After eating, they sat for a while and enjoyed the sounds coming from the slave quarters. Loud laughter could be heard along with sporadic spiritual singing. The soft ringing of cow bells flooded March with nostalgia of his childhood on his Grandpa's little farm. March smoked a final cigarette; then they headed for bed.

Chapter 10

When the chickens announced daylight was drawing near, March woke Omie and said it was time to start another day. She wanted to know if he would be back for dinner. He told her not to worry about him as he expected today would be a repeat of yesterday. He and Mr. Price still had a lot of things to see and talk about. He hoped Leroy would be meeting them with another lunch.

Omie said she and Amie still had plenty to do, but assured him tonight they would sleep inside. "I'm shore thankful fer the things that were left in the house, 'specially the iron double bedstead. I throwed that stinky old mattress away that was in there. It was filled with moss anyway, warn't fitting to sleep on. We's got our feather tick to sleep on," Omie said.

Amie was up, and they had a hasty breakfast of flapjacks along with some milk. March bid them good-bye and went to meet Mr. Price.

Mr. Price was waiting for him and said, "March let's have a look at those mules and wagon and see if we can reach an agreement on a price for them."

"Yes, Sir, Leroy has already turned them in with the other mules, and the wagon is sitting by the house."

Mr. Price yelled, "Leroy! Get yourself out here. You better not be sleeping."

"Naw, Suh, Marser Price. I's up. I's been up for a long time."

"I better not catch you sleeping after it's light enough to see. Put Mr. March's mules in a stall. We'll be back in a minute."

"Yas, Suh, Marser Price. I's gonna ketch dem right now."

Mr. Price said, "Leroy's a good hand, but you have to keep the fear in him. Now, let's look at that wagon."

Mr. Price looked the wagon and plows over and then they returned to the barn. Leroy had the mules in a stall, and Mr. Price had him turn them into a smaller pen so he could look them over well. Mr. Price looked at their teeth, checked their feet and ran his hand over their withers all the time saying, "Ugh huh," to himself. March could tell Mr. Price knew what he was looking for. He soon turned to March and said, "March, you have a fine pair of mules; you have taken good care of them. I like a man who takes care of his animals. I figure that the mules and the wagon along with the two plows ought to be worth, oh, say four hundred and fifty dollars. Any more than that, I couldn't use them. What do you say?"

March was more than pleased with that figure. He was surprised that Mr. Price was offering him so much. He replied, "You have yourself a deal. I'm indebted to you."

"Fine, fine. Now let's mount up; we still have a lot to see and many more things to discuss. I want to leave in the morning. I have to go back to Georgia and then on to New York."

They spent the remainder of the day discussing different aspects of the operation and seeing the balance of the land and crops. When they returned at dark, Mr. Price said to March, "There is one final instruction I have for you. I don't have any idea when I will be back, but I will be in touch by mail. I will require a written report once a week detailing the general health of the farm. It doesn't have to be extensive. If you need to make any major purchases, I will have to approve. You may, as I told you, buy minor emergency supplies in Monticello. I also require you to keep a daily journal describing all the happenings here, the weather each day, how much rain, etc. Also, keep me advised of the health and welfare of the workers, and any repairs made or needed, and more importantly, the progress of the crops. You have the journal of the former overseer, just use it as a guide. Mr. McCloud, I pride myself on being a good judge of character. I'm of the opinion that you are all you seem to be. I'm leaving you with a monstrous burden to shoulder, but I'm confident you can meet that challenge. Please don't do anything to make me have to reconsider. Now, I will bid you good night. I must leave early tomorrow."

With that he turned and faded into the shadows. March felt a pride in himself, but at the same time realized the magnitude of his responsibilities to El Destino and to his family. Before he went home he looked up Leroy and said to him. "Leroy, for a while, until I can find my way around, I want you to have two horses saddled and waiting in the morning. I want you to ride with me. Show me the way to all the fields and teach me their names and the names of the crew leaders."

"Yas, Suh, Marser Cloud, you can depend on Leroy. I'll have them waiting, just as you say."

When March reached home there was a lamp burning inside the house. Omie was busy at the stove preparing supper. He looked about and was amazed at the change that had taken place. The house was spotless and felt like a home--his home. Amie said, "Well, Pa, what do you think of the place now that we have hit all cleaned up?"

"Amie, you and your Ma have done worked a miracle on this old place. It's so pretty I don't think a hog would even want to live here anymore. Why, I reckon I'll have to get a bath in the pond before ya'll will let me come in. I bet Mr. Price would be surprised and pleased. Now then, can a hongry man get some vittles here? If I cain't, I'll fire you both and get me another cook. As of now you are looking at the boss of El Destino."

Omie said, "You may be the boss out there, but in here I'm the boss, and don't you ferget it. Now get yourself washed up if you intend to set and eat with decent folk."

"Yes, Ma'am."

While they were eating, March detailed the day's events to them. He told them Mr. Price would be leaving early tomorrow morning. March related his plans for tomorrow and the next few days. He was immensely proud of his new position. They were just as pleased as he was.

They discussed the issue of school for Amie. She pleaded to be allowed to stay at home. "Amie, you know how we feel about you getting some schooling. You also know I promised Mr. Price you would be going. I think he paid me a lot more fer them mules than they were worth just so's we could pay your tuition. Besides, you won't be far away. You'll be able to come home every weekend. At school you'll have friends. As soon as I get the time we'll go into Monticello and make all the arrangements. I know that your Ma agrees with me; ain't that so, Omie?"

"Amie, darling, I do think hit's best. Why, you be almost thirteen, and you need to be out and about, not stuck out here away from everybody."

"Well, I ain't a'going to like hit," Amie mumbled.

March was up early. When he got to the barn, Mr. Price was there already. "Good morning, March. I'm just leaving. I will leave the horse at the livery stable; you can send Leroy to bring him back. Here is a check for the mules and equipment. I don't think you will have any problems cashing it at the bank. I will be expecting your first report by the time I get to New York. Good luck to you." With those final words, Mr. Price mounted and rode for town.

"Leroy, you ready to go?"
"Yas, Suh, Marser Cloud, I's ready. Where you wants to go fust?"
"We'll go to the field where everybody's hoeing."

March managed most days to come home for his noon meals. Then it was back to the fields. He was careful to see how the work was done and to see that it was progressing satisfactorily. He found little to complain about.

After a week he had little trouble finding his way. He then wrote his first report to Mr. Price. The next morning Leroy hitched the buggy for them, and they went straight to the post office and mailed it.

Their next stop was the bank where March opened an account and deposited Mr. Price's check. The owner of the bank looked at him and said, "I heard about Mr. Price hiring you, Mr. McCloud. Welcome to Monticello, and thank you for putting your money in my bank. I will take good care of it for you. Now then, if you need anything you just let me know."

March thought to himself, "That ain't what he would say if'n I had asked fer a loan a'fore I put that check into his bank."

Chapter 11

After leaving the bank, they went to the academy to make arrangements for Amie's schooling. The headmaster answered all their questions to their satisfaction. Amie was to start classes the first day of the week. Her tuition was paid, and she was taken on a tour of the school that included the living quarters. Amie was apprehensive about being away from her parents for the first time but resigned herself to her fate. Before they left, it was decided that Amie would report on Sunday afternoon to begin her studies on the next Monday. Thus was set into motion the making of Amie, the uneducated and shy creature, into Amie, the sure and poised young lady she was to become.

In the few days of freedom she had left, Amie familiarized herself with El Destino by accompanying her father on his daily rounds. She had ridden a mule, of course, but never a horse. At first, she was afraid and kept him to a walk. Soon she became acclimated to the more spirited horse and began to enjoy the speed and agility of her mount. In an astonishingly short time she was riding well.

Sunday morning came all too quickly for Amie. As she packed her belongings to start school, fear overcame her. She begged to be allowed to stay at home. March and Omie consoled her, managing to calm her.

Noon time came, and they started for Monticello in the buggy. They were at last riding in style. No wagon would deposit this young lady on campus for all to laugh at. No, Sir, she would arrive in style in a carriage drawn by a matched set of bay horses stepping along at a brisk pace.

When their carriage arrived at the door of the dormitory it was met by the housemother and several of the girls. Amie was welcomed and hustled off to unpack; she barely had time to say good-bye. March told her the buggy would be waiting for her on Friday afternoon to return her to El Destino. After saying a quick good-bye, they took a short drive around town, then headed home.

Omie was heartsick for Amie. She felt her absence much more than March, now that she was alone. March was busy from sun-up until sun-down. Omie resigned herself and started a garden. It would take her mind off Amie and provide fresh vegetables for their table. That first week seemed a month long.

On Friday, Leroy hitched the buggy and drove Omie to fetch Amie. When they entered Monticello, Leroy had the team at a brisk trot. When they rounded the courthouse, Omie could see the townspeople looking at her with keen interest. Some waved to her. She waved in return. Omie felt ill at ease riding in such a fine carriage. Having a driver made it even worse. Leroy didn't mind, though. He sat ram-rod straight and touched the horses with the buggy whip for more speed.

They swept up to the doors of the academy just as the girls came flooding out. Amie was the first one out. She ran to meet Omie with a cry of, "I shore am glad to see you, Ma. Let's go home!" When she settled in her seat and Leroy put the horses into a gallop for home Amie said, "Ma, gimmie a dip of snuff. I ain't had nary one since Sunday. They won't let us dip snuff or smoke a'tall."

Omie gave her a dip and said, "You had better quit dipping snuff or you'll get into trouble."

"I'll try, Ma."

When they arrived at El Destino, Amie could hardly wait to tell March all about school. She was running over with things to say about it and the people she had met. She had made lots of friends and was even invited to stay over the weekend with some. She explained to March and Omie the school curriculum. Along with reading, writing and arithmetic, one also learned to be a lady. Social graces were foremost on the agenda.

Amie was relieved to be at home with her parents and away from the stress of school and new people. She admitted to herself that after a day or two she had begun to enjoy her new surroundings. Still she was torn between staying at El Destino and returning to school. When Sunday dinner was over she reluctantly hopped onto the buggy for the return trip to school.

Because Amie had a limited amount of schooling, she was far behind most of the other children. That made her the center of attention. Fortunately the teachers were sympathetic and wouldn't allow her to be teased.

The weeks seemed to merge one into the other, and soon it was time for the fall holidays. Amie had adjusted to a new life away from home. She was spending some of her week-ends with friends from school. Her life had taken a dramatic turn.

March received a letter informing him to expect Mr. Price around the first of November. He was instructed to have the house readied for him and his family. March was anxious to know how Mr. Price would assess his work. Most of the crops had been harvested. The rest would be in the barns by the time Mr. Price and his family arrived. In

March's opinion it had been a good year. The yields were better than he had ever experienced in South Carolina. He hoped Mr. Price would be satisfied.

He needn't have worried. When Mr. Price arrived and had a chance to estimate the harvest, he was more than pleased. He was generous in his praise to March.

Mr. Price had brought his family with him to El Destino. March was surprised to learn his children were much older than he expected. He then learned they were Mr. Price's stepchildren, two girls about Amie's age. They secluded themselves in the house and were seldom seen.

Amie longed for company, but was told by the girls they weren't allowed to play with her. For the first time Amie experienced segregation from her own kind. She was heartbroken.

Omie tried to soothe Amie as best she could by explaining that the hired help didn't associate with the employer and his family. Amie wasn't satiated and wanted to spend her vacation with one of her school friends. It was decided that might be the best solution. Amie's brief encounter with her "betters" ended abruptly.

Mr. Price and his family stayed through the Christmas holidays. They left after New Year's Day. He had high praise for the way March was running the plantation and offered no advice. He said his business needed his full attention, and he might not be back again that year. March was to proceed with another year's activities just as in the previous one. March had full confidence in his abilities and pride in all his accomplishments. Omie felt no less pride in March herself, and she let him know it in every way possible.

The year 1822 was coming to an end when Mr. Price came again, this time without his family. He only stayed for a few days and was gone before the New Year was celebrated. Amie was well into her thirteenth year and was rapidly developing into a woman. She had grown taller, nearly as tall as her mother. She was losing the gangling locomotion of a teenager. Amie was going to be a stunner.

Already she was the most popular girl on campus. Her presence was in demand at all the parties given by the parents of her classmates. Needless to say, March and Omie were immensely proud of her. They, of course, could not host parties at El Destino but from time to time did have picnic outings or watermelon cuttings for Amie and her friends.

Being the overseer did have certain advantages, and the job certainly was looked upon as one of the upper positions in the county. From time to time March and Omie received invitations to attend social gatherings. They declined whenever possible. They realized they neither had the skills nor the wherewithal for socializing, and so made their excuses, leaving it up to Amie to represent them. And represent them, she did! As her reputation grew, so did the name of Mr. and Mrs. McCloud of El Destino.

The McClouds were proud of Amie's accomplishments in school. Her grades had soared after her first six months. Her teachers reported that she was sure to become a very important person in the community. With those lofty pronouncements, the year 1823 ended.

Mr. Price made another brief appearance that same year. His business interests kept him in New York and other parts of the world. He expressed total confidence in March's ability and left all decision making to him.

He raised March's pay fifty dollars each year. March and Omie were overjoyed. For the first time they began to feel they had a future. Since March had taken over, El Destino enjoyed the best crops ever. March's status was enhanced and so was El Destino's.

In 1824, Amie had grown into a mature beauty of fifteen. Without doubt she was the belle of the county. She was a far cry from the gangling, snuff dipping, uneducated backwoods girl who entered school in 1821. She was courted by all the local dandies who begged for her hand in marriage.

She rebuffed them all until she met a young banker from Tallahassee, named James Weston. He won her heart. They were married in the latter part of 1824.

But alas, fate intervened. Just as the new year's holidays ended, while on their way to supper one evening, as they stepped into the street, a freight wagon careened around the corner, its team wild, and the driver unable to control them. James threw Amie aside and took the full impact of the wheel. The wagon continued on, out of control. It almost hit several more people before it could be stopped.

Amie threw herself on her dying husband, cradling his head in her lap. "Help me; someone, please," she cried.

A doctor was summoned, and James was carried to a nearby hotel. Amie was beside herself and inconsolable, so much so the doctor was hardly able to tend his patient.

Amie refused to leave James for even an instant. All the while she held his hand and confessed her love for him without ceasing. Word was sent to March and Omie, and they came at once. They tried, on the advice of the doctor, to get Amie away from James' bedside, but to no avail.

Three days later James died. Amie was so distressed she was unable to attend the funeral. She had to be sedated for days. She was so stricken with her loss that she vowed to kill herself and be buried beside her beloved James. She refused to eat or care for herself. She cried constantly and declined to see any of her friends. March, by necessity, had to be away much of the time, but Omie stayed at her side comforting her as best she could, wiping her tears and washing her face.

Weeks went by before Amie began to mend. She started taking regular meals again and took note of her bedraggled appearance. She consented to return to El Destino with her parents. For a long time she refused to see anyone or take part in any social gatherings. Omie and March lent her as much support as they could. Gradually the grief Amie suffered began to lessen.

Fully a year went by before Amie regained her composure enough to show herself in public. Slowly, she allowed friends to come and visit her. She spent most of her time riding alone on the endless trails of El Destino. Her father accompanied her whenever he could.
When James was killed, he and Amie were in the finishing stages of building a new house. After James' death, Amie turned over its progress and the care of a modest interest in the local bank she received from her husband's estate to an attorney to administer for her. She lamented to Omie that she would never love another and would always remain a widow. Omie tried to assure her that one day she would get over the hurt and find someone else to love. "Oh, Ma, I just couldn't." But time heals all wounds, especially those of the young.

Chapter 12

Toward the end of 1825, Mr. Price returned to El Destino with one of his sisters, Mabelle Thurston, and her two daughters, who were near Amie's age, and his elderly aunt. He informed the McClouds that his wife was sick and preferred to stay in New York to be near her doctor.

This time Amie was not ignored. She soon became fast friends with Georgina and Merle Thurston. Their father was in the steel business in Pittsburgh. Amie began to think life just might be worth living again. The three of them spent their days horseback riding, participating in casual picnics, and attending balls given at one plantation or another.

Soon, El Destino became a social place. Amie's friends were welcomed by Georgina and Merle. Lights blazed far into the night. Music filled the air while couples whirled around the grand ballroom. Mr. Price approved of it all.

Invitations were extended to all the gentry. They were received and accepted. In turn the recipients issued their own invitations. Life had come to El Destino in a big way, and Amie McCloud Weston was in the midst of it all.

Through it all March and Omie shook their heads in wonderment. They sat in their little overseer's house and watched and listened. They were politely acknowledged but uninvited, for which they were grateful.

Again, Amie was the belle of the ball, but now she had rivals. The Thurston sisters were, after all, rich and beautiful. Their uncle was the master of El Destino, holder of vast and sundry worldwide interests. When this became evident, the Thurstons naturally became the magnet that drew most attention. Georgina and Merle relished the rivalry between the two of them and Amie.

In 1825 the world around Jefferson and Leon Counties took on new meaning. Nearby Tallahassee boasted a hundred houses with a population of over three hundred people. It had a bank, a newspaper and many other businesses. The Territorial Governor, William P. Duval, was in residence.

John Gamble, the Bellamy brothers, and General LaFayette were also part of the scene. Then a new person appeared; it was none other than royalty, Prince Achille Murat, the Napoleonic exile. Never had so many men of consequence gathered in such a backward place. The atmosphere was charged with excitement. What did it all mean? Great expectations arose. Some were fulfilled, others loomed imminent.

Throughout the year, every weekend a ball was held at one of the many plantations. Amie was sure to receive an invitation, along with the Thurston sisters. Amie was courted all over again and inundated with proposals of marriage that she demurely declined. Prince Murat was seen in her company quite frequently. It was rumored marriage was possible, indeed imminent. It never happened because suddenly, who should appear on the scene but the great grandniece of the first president, George Washington.

Like Amie, she was a recent widow. Catherine Daingerfield Willis Gray was her name and a wealthy socialite in her own right. Here, she met the heir to a

Napoleonic fortune, if he could only collect it without losing his head in the bargain. In just a short time they were wed. They started construction on their plantation home west of Tallahassee. They called it "Lipona." Prince Murat, until his marriage, had been living in a log cabin. He reveled in the simple life of an ordinary country man, living in squalor and filth, seemingly loving it.

If Amie was surprised or hurt by this sudden turn of events, she didn't show it. Life for her continued in a whirl of encounters with both old and new acquaintances. Rumors flew from time to time that she was easy, a trollop. Those starting the rumors were never a part of her life.

The good life intensified at El Destino.

March and Omie went about life in their usual way. Amie drifted further away from them. Oh, she still loved them, but their ways were no longer her ways. She in no way denied her parentage or sought to explain her sudden outburst of folksy sayings. Occasionally she even indulged in a dip of snuff, but always with discretion, making sure no one saw her. She began to travel with the Thurstons. She was invited to spend summers with them in the Addirondaks, the coast of Maine, or Massachusetts.

As time went by, her world was expanded with the aid of the Thurstons. Amie was considered a part of the family because of her close friendship with Merle and Georgina. When the Thurstons toured Europe, naturally Amie was invited. True, she had some money of her own, but not enough to support the lavish splendor in which she found herself.

In Europe, too, Amie captured the hearts of her suitors. Her rivals were still the same, Merle and Georgina Thurston. The three thrived on the competition. She received numerous proposals that would have culminated in a life of comfort and splendor. She declined them all.

When the long holidays ended in Europe, Amie returned to El Destino resuming her life as if she had never been away.

One day as Amie and Omie sat reminiscing, Amie said, "Do you remember what I said when we were traveling through Georgia? Remember, I said when I became rich we would travel and eat in all the fancy places. Well, I'm not rich, but I do have some money from my banking interest, along with the rent monies from my house in Tallahassee that I have saved. I think it's time we all took a trip. Where would you like to go?"

"Oh, Amie, I ain't never had no hankering to travel. I've always been content to be where you and March are. Sometimes, I think of my Ma and Pa a'way out yonder in Kansas. I don't even know if they are still alive. I would like to see them one more time 'fore I die."

"Then, to Kansas we'll go. Get a letter in the mail. Tell them we are coming. Tell them as soon as we hear from them, we'll be on our way."

"Oh, I don't know, Amie. Hit's such a long way. I don't think March could leave this place long enough to go way out there."

"Then, just you and I will go. I'm not going to take no for an answer. Get a letter in the mail today."

Chapter 13

March couldn't go with them, but one fine spring day in 1829, Omie and Amie sailed on one of those ships that the wind blows! They boarded in St. Marks and debarked in New Orleans.

Met in New Orleans by friends of Amie, they spent a week as honored guests, eating in many of the fine restaurants. Balls were held in Amie's honor, and Omie was included. Omie, dressed in her fine new wardrobe, felt out of place but managed to be gracious and smiled through it all.

From New Orleans, they took a riverboat to St. Louis. There they were met by more of Amie's friends. They were wined and dined in a sumptuous manner. Nothing was too good for Amie and her wonderful Mother.

After a time they were on their way overland in a chartered stagecoach to Kansas City. Once again, they were welcomed by friends of Amie as long lost sisters.

Omie was overwhelmed. The pomp, the ceremony, the lavishness of it all. It was a fairy tale, and Omie loved it! Was this the way rich folks lived all the time? What would March think? Would he believe it if she told him? Will Ma and Pa believe such a tale?

In Kansas City they hired a buggy for the last few miles of their trip. They passed through a small village where they received directions to the Whaley's (Omie's Ma and Pa, Dodge and Emma) homestead.

The land was treeless, filled with long waving grass. The wind moaned and whistled as it wrung and twisted the tall buffalo grass. "Oh, Ma, it's so lonesome here," Amie cried.

"Hit do seem like the end of the world. I'd druther be back home with March."

They topped a rise in the land, and there before them stood a small shack between two hills. In the distance they could see clothes waving in the wind, hanging from a wire with a prop in the middle. In the yard was a wagon. Attached to the house was a lean-to. Beside the wagon a man and woman stood looking their way.

When they got closer the man and woman took a few steps toward them with expectant faces. Amie stopped the horses. They sat and looked at the wrinkled and bent old couple. They resembled corn shuck dolls. Omie was so overcome with emotion, she could only sob, "Mama, Papa, hit's me, Omie. Don't you know me? This is Amie, yore grand-youngun."

They got down from the buggy. The two old folks came toward them with arms open, shouting with joy. "Omie, is hit really you? Thank you, Lord, we'uns didn't know if we would ever see you no more. Thank you, Lord; thank you, Lord. Dodge, come hug yore youngun and yore grand-youngun!"

Dodge enclosed Omie and Amie with skinny arms and knarled hands, hands that had been twisted by age and hard work. His Adam's apple bobbed up and down with emotion.

"Omie, we's thought of you many-a-day since we left Caroline. When Emma and me got yore letter, why we never once thought we'd see you here in our yard. God has been good to us though, and here you are." They cried and hugged each other for a while, then went and sat on the edge of the porch. A tired old dog opened one eye, looked at them, then went back to sleep.

Dodge and Emma treated Amie as if she was a precious jewel, lost and now reclaimed. Every few minutes she was treated to a hug or had her hands squeezed. They would exclaim, "Ain't she just the purtyest thing in the whole world?" Amie looked in wonder at the grandparents she had never seen. Looking at her grandma, even at her extreme age, she saw a little of herself. Emma and Omie held hands and reminisced about the past while Amie looked and listened.

Several days passed, and then they all visited Kansas City for three whole days, and Amie paid the expenses. They dined in all the fine restaurants and stayed in the finest hotel. Dodge and Emma were embarrassed to be seen living so extravagantly. Why, in their whole lifetime, they had never spent half as much on themselves as Amie showered on them in those three days!

After their fling in Kansas City, the farm seemed a serene part of heaven to Dodge and Emma. It had been for them "a once in a lifetime" experience. They would remember it forever, but it wasn't their way of life. They were more at ease in their own home.

Omie and Amie tried to entice them to come with them to Monticello, but Dodge said, "I reckon me and Emma will die right here in this little shack. Hit ain't much, I reckon, but we's content." Emma smiled at Dodge and squeezed his hand.

A few more days, then sadly Omie and Amie made ready to leave. Tears flowed from Omie's parents' wrinkled old eyes. They knew they would never see their

Omie and Amie again this side of heaven. Amie and Omie cried tears of grief as they said farewell.

Left standing on the porch, they were like two old scarecrows holding each other for support. They were withered and bent with age, scarred by a lifetime of toil and deprivation. They waved to Omie and Amie until they could no longer see through the tears that filled their tired old eyes.

Omie had Amie stop on top of a rise. She got out of the buggy and stood looking back at her Ma and Pa for one final time. "Thank you, God, fer letting me be with them one more time. Please take good care of them fer us." Omie lifted her hand in a final salute as the buggy rolled away.

When they returned to El Destino, Amie established herself in Tallahassee and became active in the affairs of the bank where she held a partnership inherited from her husband. Of course, she was only a minor partner without real say in the running of it. Besides, she was only a child, not even twenty-one yet. Still, Amie insisted on learning how it all worked. She was tolerated but not encouraged.

Soon her enthusiasm for banking flagged as her youthful energy surged once more to the forefront. She stopped going to the bank, much to the relief of the senior partners.

She turned to teaching school for a time. That, too, soon bored her. She was in a quandary about what to do with herself. She was still the most sought after young lady in Jefferson and Leon Counties. Why was she bored?

She drifted; then abruptly left for New York City and sought out her old friends.

In New York City, she joined the Thurston sisters for long cruises up and down the East Coast. Glamour and excitement abounded, mingling with the rich and famous. Hardly had one party ended when another started. How she loved the attention that was lavished upon her. Still, somewhere down deep within her, there lingered a feeling of emptiness.

She left New York City and again found herself in Europe. She joined in with the same old crowd she had known before. It was as if she had taken a short nap and awakened to yet another party. The same clownish faces, the same proposals. While they still thrilled her, there was that old nagging feeling deep in her soul saying to her, "You don't belong here. These are not your people." She missed her father and mother, missed their folksy ways. She longed for a pot of peas, some grits, a sweet potato and, secretly, a dip of snuff.

She sailed for home. She had been gone too long.

Chapter 14

In 1833, Amie was almost twenty-five years old when she returned to El Destino and her family. Her father and mother, she realized, were beginning to show their ages. Those hard years of barely having enough to eat, those lean years of uncertainties had taken their tolls. Still, they were robust, without chronic ailments she could detect. They welcomed her home as always; she felt at peace, as when she was a child.

She gorged on the foods she had missed so much. She rode everyday beside her father. She became familiar once again with El Destino and its inhabitants.

The big house was silent and had been for the last three years. Mr. Price wrote that his wife had died from her illness. He was terribly busy with his many business ventures. He didn't know when he would come again. The house sat unused, collecting dust.

Amie was content to sit and collect dust too. That same year, 1833, a new bank was chartered in Tallahassee, Union Bank. It issued two million dollars in "Faith Bonds," whatever that was. Amie's bank merged with it.

Suddenly, money was plentiful. The bank loaned to anyone and everyone. Some worried the bank was on shaky ground. Others saw it another way. After all, none other than Daniel Webster himself had given it the all clear. Amie had no opinion or say.

As the money flowed, so too did enthusiasm. Plantation houses re-emerged from the gloom that had overtaken them. Lights glowed brightly from every room, music wafted over manicured gardens while couples strolled along gardenia scented walks. Invitations sealed in aromatic envelopes and delivered by servants were sent and received with regularity. All was well again in "de land of cotton."

Amie slipped back into it as naturally as a bird to its nest. Land was bought and sold with the help of the banks. Each time a piece was sold, new money would be borrowed on its appreciated value which was far higher than its true value. Some predicted doom, but were ignored.

The good times rolled on. Amie re-occupied her home in Tallahassee. Once more she enjoyed the limelight, socializing with the elite of society.

As new settlers flooded into Florida, friction flared again between whites and Indians. It erupted into the second Indian War in 1835. There was a move to exterminate the "Red Devils" once and for all. "Send them to Oklahoma; better yet kill them all," seemed to be the sentiment.

Most of the Indians had already fled to the extreme southern part of Florida to escape being rounded up and forced to leave their ancestral homelands. A few holdouts remained, hiding and skulking in the deep hammocks. They would conduct lightning raids on outlying homesteads and then disappear. Hawk, who had saved Omie's life when she was snake bitten, was one such holdout. Unlike some of the other Indians though, he did not seek confrontation. His only desire was to live in peace, preferring solitude.

So far, El Destino had escaped the wrath visited upon some outlying homesteads. Then in the nearby hamlet of Lamont, a family was attacked and killed and their house burned. The Governor sent troops to capture or kill those responsible. They were unsuccessful.

March kept his gun handy and the workers on the look-out for any sign of Indians. The Army returned to Florida determined this time to round up all the Indians. Amie feared for her parents, isolated as they were, twenty miles from Tallahassee without any protection. She moved in with them over their objection. "At least I can be an extra set of eyes and give warning," she argued.

Chapter 15

Then, without warning, Mr. Price came to El Destino. With him were his business partner and brother-in-law, Mr. Robert Ireland, Mr. Ireland's wife Nora, who was also Mr. Price's sister, and their son, Van. Edna Sutter, Mr. Price's eldest sister, also came with the Irelands.

Van Ireland was a tall, muscular man about Amie's age. Amie had just ridden up when their carriage arrived from Monticello. "Amie, hello. Come and meet my guests. They will be staying for a few days at El Destino," yelled Mr. Price.

"What a surprise, Mr. Price! My father didn't mention you coming."

"Yes, I know. I'm sorry for that. I decided to come on the spur of the moment. I knew we would be here before a letter could arrive."

Mr. Price made introductions all around. He introduced Amie as his own daughter: "At least I wish she was my daughter," he said. Mrs. Ireland looked askance at him upon hearing his declaration.

Van had not taken his eyes off Amie since his arrival. She was wearing riding clothes that revealed all her attributes to their best advantage. He stepped forward and said, "Miss Amie, that is a beautiful horse you are riding. I love to ride. May I have the pleasure of riding with you tomorrow?"

Amie replied, "This horse belongs to Mr. Price. With his permission I would be delighted, Mr. Ireland."

"Please, call me Van." Then turning to Mr. Price, he asked, "Uncle Dan, could we have your permission?"

"Amie never needs my permission for anything. As for you, Van, I shall be watching you closely, you scalawag. Ride as much and as often as you please."

"Thank you, Uncle Dan. Miss Amie, may I call at nine?"

"Nine will do nicely, thank you. Now I must find my father and let him know Mr. Price is here."

"Thank you, Amie, and would you please tell Martha we are here and to come right away?"

Amie hurried away to find Martha, then mounted and rode in search of her father. A tingle surged through her body when she thought of Van Ireland. "I think I'm going to enjoy our ride," she confided to herself.

When she found March and told him the news, he quickly mounted his horse and together they rode back to the house. They turned their mounts over to Leroy. Amie hurried home to inform Omie of the unexpected arrival of the owner of El Destino, while March sought Mr. Price. As she hurried past the big house, she could see Van sitting on the porch watching her. He raised his hand in greeting as she hurried on. She acknowledged him with a smile. There it was again, that little tingle, "Well, well, well, Mr. Ireland---Van."

Next morning Amie met Van coming from the stables leading her favorite horse and a black gelding for himself. "Good morning, Miss Amie. I'm an early riser, so I had Leroy saddle your favorite horse and one for me. I hope that was all right?"

"Yes, of course. Thank you. If you like, we can take a tour of the work in progress."

"Lead on, Miss Amie. I shall try to follow."

Amie led off at a trot; soon Van came alongside. As they rode, he questioned her about the plantation and its operation. She saw soon enough that Van was no farmer by his lack of comprehension. Van soon tired of seeing field hands, hoeing, and cotton growing. He suggested they return home. Amie agreed and spurred her mount ahead.

When they turned the horses over to Leroy, Van asked Amie, "Will you be having lunch with Mr. Price?"

She replied, "No, I will be eating with my mother. Then I must carry my father his lunch."

"May I ride with you?"

"Yes, if you like."

Before Amie finished eating, there was a knock on the door. When she answered, there stood Van. He excused the intrusion by saying he didn't know just when she might be ready, so he thought he had better inquire. Amie asked him in and introduced him to her mother. While Van visited with her mother, Amie prepared lunch for March. When she finished making sandwiches, she turned to Van and said, "All set. Are you ready?"

"Yes," he replied, then politely excused himself. They hurried to the stables. This time Leroy had two different horses saddled and waiting for them.

They rode to the field where Amie knew her father would be waiting. While March ate his lunch, Amie and Van sat with him. Van plied him with questions about the operation of such a vast farm. Between bites of food, March answered his questions as best he could.

When he finished his lunch, he excused himself saying, "I must go back to work. Have a pleasant ride and be careful. Don't ride too fer off. There's been some evidence of Indians near the creek in the last few days."

Van and Amie rode to a place where there was a spring with lots of shade. They loosed the cinches on the saddles and let the horses drink. Afterward they dropped the reins to the ground, freeing the horses to graze. Amie knew they wouldn't wander far. They refreshed themselves with a cool drink, then sat down for a long talk. Van had a million questions to ask, most of them about Amie.

Amie talked for awhile but, as a woman will, soon steered the conversation to Van. And, as a man will, he was only too eager to disclose his entire life. He told her of his work, his friends, his dreams and aspirations. He was related to the Thurston family and knew many of the same people Amie knew in the North.

When the day was far spent they mounted their horses and slowly rode back. Upon reaching the stables, Van wanted to know if he could see her again tomorrow. Maybe they could pack a lunch and ride to Tallahassee or Monticello. Amie agreed and they parted.

Van thought Amie was just about the prettiest girl he had ever seen. That night he cornered Mr. Price and inundated him with questions concerning Amie. Mr. Price told him the story of the former overseer getting himself killed and of the chance meeting with March at a time when he was desperate for someone to oversee El Destino. He told Van how March had stepped in and made El Destino prosper.

He praised March for his innovations in several areas. He explained how March came to him with a proposal to build a sawmill. It would supply El Destino's lumber needs. In addition, between crops the mill would meet the needs of the community.

He related to Van how March constructed ditches to channel water away from low spots and store it to augment the creek in times of low water. Now the gristmill and sawmill operated from the same power source. Mr. Price was long in his praise for March. He was especially proud of Amie. He revealed Amie's many accomplishments since coming to El Destino. He told Van of Amie's short marriage and her husband's accidental death in Tallahassee. He disclosed to Van, Amie's share in the Union Bank of Tallahassee and of her home there.

Later that evening at dinner, Van narrated his day to his mother and father, gushing in his assessment of Amie and her family. He told them he and Amie would be going on a picnic and perhaps a ride to Tallahassee tomorrow. He asked, "Uncle Dan, would it be all right if Martha made us a lunch?"
"Of course, it will be all right. Just tell Martha; she will prepare it for you."
"Thank you, Uncle Dan."
Van's mother said, "Van, I don't think it's proper for you to be seeing so much of that girl. After all, she is just the hired help's daughter."
"Well, what's wrong with that, Mother?" Van asked.
"What's wrong with it? I'll tell you what's wrong with it. She is below our class. I wouldn't want it known that my son is seeing her."
"Mother, Uncle Dan thinks highly of her and her father too." His mother just looked sour. Mr. Price and Mr. Ireland kept silent.
Mrs. Ireland said, "We shall discuss this matter later."

After dinner, Van found Martha and asked her to make a picnic basket for him and Miss Amie. Martha replied with a big smile, "I sho nuff will, Mr. Ireland. I sho hopes y'all has a good time."

Just before they went to bed, Mr. Ireland let his wife know he thought she was wrong about Amie. "I don't think you should have brought it up in front of Mr. Price. Dan has high regards for her and her family, even though they are, as you say "hired help," besides Van is not a child, you know."
"I don't want him getting too close to that woman. The next thing we know he will be wanting to bring her to dinner, and Lord knows what else. There are more

suitable young ladies among our acquaintances who are held in high regard. I don't want it known that he associates with someone beneath our social standing."

Mr. Ireland had been through it all before, so he dropped the subject.

At breakfast next morning, before Mr. Price came in, Van's mother again broached the subject with Van. "I absolutely forbid you to associate with that servant girl."

"Mother, she isn't a servant girl. She is part owner of the Union Bank, and she owns her own home in Tallahassee. Uncle Dan thinks the world of her. If you pursue the subject, it will make for a most uncomfortable situation. I intend to go on this outing today regardless of what you might say. Amie has promised to arrange a dance in my honor, with Uncle Dan's blessing. Furthermore, it will be given here at El Destino. All of Uncle Dan's friends will be in attendance. I suggest, Mother, you not make a fuss over it."

Turning to Van's father she said, "Are you going to allow your son to talk to his mother that way?"

"Now, now, Mother, Van is right. We are guests here. Dan is very fond of Amie and her family. We mustn't do anything that might appear to disagree with our host."

The conversation ended abruptly when Mr. Price came in.

Van and Amie decided not to ride to Tallahassee or Monticello either. Instead they rode to the head of the Wacissa River. There were several couples swimming and a horseshoe game in progress when they arrived. Amie introduced Van to her friends, then they joined in the fun by taking a swim.

Several springs spew millions of gallons of pure, clean water that form the majestic Wacissa River. It flows with crystal clarity for about twenty miles, where it empties into the Gulf of Mexico. "It's a popular place; people come from all around to picnic and swim," Amie said to Van.

At noon, Amie and Van enjoyed their lunch under a massive oak tree. Afterwards, they joined in a game of horseshoes. While they played, Amie outlined her plans for the dance to be given in Van's honor and invited the group to attend.

The discussion then turned to a "Float Trip" to Goose Pasture to see the canal being dug by slaves. "It's planned for Saturday. Why don't you and Van come along?"

Amie said, "I would like to see the canal. Mr. Price is furnishing some of the workers."

Van asked, "What about this canal?"

Amie replied, "For a long time there has been a need for a better way to get the cotton produced in this area and south Georgia to the coast. There, waiting ships deliver it to markets around the world. Until now, it had to be hauled by wagon to St. Marks. For most farmers, that is a long and hard trip. If they could float it down the Wacissa River, then it would be much easier and quicker. The barges that deliver the cotton could then return with goods off-loaded in St. Marks. All the big landowners are contributing workers. I think the state government of Florida is involved too."

Van said to Amie, "That sounds very interesting. Let's go with them."

"I don't know, Van. It would take all day to float to Goose Pasture. We would have to spend the night there, and the mosquitoes will be terrible."

"Oh, come on, Amie. It will be fun and a real adventure."

Amie and Van promised to go. They would meet the others early Saturday morning. Arrangements for the boats had already been made. The only thing left to do was to send some wagons ahead to Goose Pasture for the return trip. When all the plans were made, Amie and Van returned to El Destino.

When Van told his mother of their plans, she was fit to be tied. She suggested to Mr. Ireland that they pack up and leave El Destino at once. "Why, the very idea, going off on a river and staying in the woods all night! Besides being dangerous, it's immoral, unmarried folks away from home without chaperons. I told you that girl was just trash. Our son shouldn't be seen with her."

Van's father, after a lengthy argument, was able to smooth her ruffled feathers some, but not enough for her consent. She said, "I shall never forgive you if anything happens to Van, Mr. Ireland."

"You forget, Mother. Van is a grown man. Besides, what can happen with all those people there?"

"You know very well what can happen. People can talk. If this gets back to our friends we'll be ruined."

"I shan't tell. Will you, Mother?"

Friday afternoon, Amie and Van packed the things they would need for the trip.

Chapter 16

Early Saturday morning, Leroy drove them to the river for the start of the float. Those going in the boats were ready. Those driving the wagons for the return trip had already left. There were eight boats with two people in each.

When they started out it was a clear day but muggy. Soon the clouds began to build, threatening rain. The wind abruptly changed from a gentle breeze to boat rocking gusts. They were not alarmed at first. Getting wet was something they were all used to.

As the storm gathered strength, the winds became stronger. They hooted and hollered. "Let her blow, let her blow!"

Amie said to the others, "Maybe we should turn back. It looks as if this might be a real storm."

They replied, "Oh, don't worry. It will soon be over, just a little old thunderstorm."

Soon the winds were really howling and the boats became unmanageable. Amie said, "We must get off the river; I believe this is a hurricane."

They took refuge amongst the huge cypress trees growing abundantly along the banks. The wind intensified, shrieking through the branches. The rain came down so hard the boats were in danger of sinking. They sought dry land. The country through which the river flows is low, boggy ground. Dry landings along the river are scarce.

Finally they were able to pull the boats from the water. They were exhausted and cold. The winds increased in velocity. The sky turned dark, blotting out the sun's light completely. Rain came down in torrents, lightning crashed around them illuminating the forest of trees briefly.

They realized they were in the midst of a real hurricane. Amie said, "We need shelter. I saw some axes in one of the boats. Get them and cut some poles and lash them between the trees. We can put the boats on them and get under them."

The men set to work with zeal. The overturned boats provided some shelter from the pounding rain but not from the wind. They were soaked, and without the sun to warm them, they were cold even though the temperature was probably eighty degrees. A fire was out of the question. They wore all the clothing they could find and sat huddled together for the comfort one finds at a time like that.

When the storm struck, those traveling in the wagons decided it was not an ordinary storm. They turned the wagons around and raced for shelter in the village of Wacissa. Their flight was hampered by trees blown helter skelter across the road.

Several times they were obliged to cut trees from their path. They experienced near misses as the tall pines swayed and fell, their shallow roots torn from the ground by the force of the wind. The horses, crazed with fear, had to be led by their halters to prevent them from running away and wrecking the wagons.

After what seemed like an eternity, they came to Wacissa, where they found shelter in a barn. As they waited for the storm to end, suddenly part of the roof disappeared.

Next, the supports began to give way. The barn leaned at a crazy angle. Everyone made a mad dash outside just as the entire barn collapsed.

Hurriedly, they sought the railroad station. It was solidly built. There they hoped to be safe. They had shelter, but the horses were exposed to flying debris and about to panic. One of the men suggested turning them loose to find their own shelter. As soon as the horses were unhitched, they raced away down the open road and in seconds were swallowed up by the rain.

The group forced their way into the station house. One exclaimed, "What a relief to be out of the wind and rain! I think we'll be safe here. My God, what do you suppose has happened to those on the river?"

"They will have to do the best they can until it's over, just like us," said another.

March had been watching the storm building up with concern. The sky turned darker and the winds started gusting, lashing the pines making them bend low to the ground. March rushed home. He said to Omie, "I'm worried. This is going to be a bad storm. I hope Amie and her friends are all right. I'll be back; I must warn Mr. Price."

When he reached the big house, he pounded on the door. Mr. Ireland opened it. March stepped inside and closed the door. "Mr. Ireland, I believe a severe storm is coming, and I wanted to let Mr. Price know." Mr. Price was just coming down the stairs and heard what he said.

He asked, "March, what can we do about it?"

"There's not much we can do, except just watch and be ready to get out of the house if it starts to go," March replied.

Mrs. Ireland screamed at her husband, "I warned you something bad was going to happen if they went off. I asked you to forbid them to go, but you wouldn't listen. You must go look for Van."

March interrupted, "Ma'am, you cain't go out in weather like this. You wouldn't get fer before you got hit by a tree or lost. You cain't see ten feet ahead of you. There ain't but one thing to do; stay put until this storm passes."

"Thank you, March, that's what we'll do. Please try to stay in touch with us," said Mr. Ireland.

"I'll do the best I can," March replied. "Right now, I'm going to put the slaves in the gin room. They will have a better chance of surviving there. Just as soon as this storm is over, we'll try to get to the river and see if we can find out what's going on with the children."

Just as soon as March left to see about the safety of the slaves, Mrs. Ireland started in again, ridiculing her husband for his lack of judgment. She was completely beside herself. Mr. Ireland began to fear for her sanity. He gave her several large drinks to try and calm her, but it only made her more excited.

Finally, Mr. Price brought a bottle of laudanum and advised Mr. Ireland to give her some. Perhaps it would make her sleep. After a time, it did, much to their relief.

Mr. Ireland felt he must apologize to Dan for his wife's bad behavior, and said, "As soon as this storm is over, we'll be leaving, Dan."

"No need for that, I understand. These things happen sometimes; think no more of it," Dan said.

March managed to get most of the people inside the gin room where he hoped they would be safe, then he went home. The wind was blowing harder than March had ever seen it blow before. The trees were swaying, the pines nearly touching the ground. Some had fallen, others had large limbs sheared off. The ground was littered with debris. Omie had a pot of coffee ready when he came in. He accepted a cup gratefully. He was thankful for the snug little house but filled with anxiety for Amie and her friends. Only God knew if they were still alive.

Amie and Van, along with all the rest of the group had endured the storm all day. Now the last pale glimmer of daylight was rapidly fading. The rain had been ceaseless, falling in torrents, whipped about by violent winds. It shrieked and moaned through the trees, punctuated by lethal crashes of lightning.

The water had risen where they were huddled. Amie began to fear they might have to take to the boats. Their faces revealed the terrible strain they were under.

Until now, they hadn't eaten anything. They had been totally absorbed with the storm. When someone suggested food, they found most of the food they had brought was in a soggy condition and not edible. Only the boiled eggs had survived. They ate those and were grateful.

Then they managed to maneuver one of the larger boats so that it gave some protection from the driving wind. It was good to have this little protection from the elements.

As the storm howled about them, Van and Amie held each other for the warmth each provided to the other. It gave comfort to know another human was near. They couldn't talk because of the roar of the wind.

Quickly the water rose and covered their refuge. From time to time Amie felt things slither about her legs. Were they fish or snakes? She knew that with the shrinking land about them all the critters inhabiting the surrounding woods would be in search of high ground as the water drove them from the low places. Amie loved adventure, but this was more than she had ever wished for.

Her thoughts turned to those driving the wagons to Goose Pasture. She hoped they were all right. What about her Father and Mother? She wondered if they were thinking of her at that moment. They wouldn't know if she was alive or dead. How were Mr. and Mrs. Ireland? She knew they must be in agony over Van. Her mind drifted, she was so tired. Even in the midst of the storm she dozed while others cried out from the fear that gripped them.

Dawn was a long time coming. The sun shining high above struggled to erase the long dark night. The wind began noticeably dropping in velocity. The rain slowed in its fury. One by one, they stirred and stretched cramped limbs and sore bodies. Then, as one, they gave thanks to God for sparing them.

When there was light enough to see, they began to plan a return to Wacissa. Amie knew with all the rain the surrounding low country would be running with water for weeks. Travel by land would be almost impossible. There didn't seem to be any reason for continuing on to Goose Pasture.

Amie and those stranded with her found some high ground alongside the river to walk on, but they worried if they left the river that any rescuers would overlook them. Their best option was to pole the boats back upstream. It would be slow going against the raging current caused by the run-off. It would take all day in their poor condition to return the few miles back to Wacissa. Being without food and exposed to the storm had robbed them of their reserves of energy.

They reasoned two could pole more effectively against the swift flowing river. They abandoned half of the boats, dragging the rest back into the fast flowing river. The boats were crowded, and the extra weight left very little freeboard. One by one they set out for Wacissa and home.

Their progress against the rushing waters was pitifully slow. Soon, blisters appeared on cramped hands. Shoulder muscles screamed for relief as the bedraggled flotilla inched forward.

Those waiting out the storm in the train depot were dry and warm. Their food supply had survived the deluge of rain, but it had been devoured long ago. They knew from the violent winds that lashed the depot, if those on the river hadn't made it to shore and found some kind of protection, they might not survive. As night descended, they could only hope and pray that their friends would survive the night.

  March and Omie spent a sleepless night. From time to time March braved the storm to check on Mr. Price and also the slaves in the gin room. The main house was holding up well, although several patches of shingles had blown off and some windows were shattered from flying debris. March covered them with quilts re-enforced with boards to keep the rain out. Mrs. Ireland, with the help of the drinks and laudanum, had been unaware of anything for a long time. Mrs. Sutter went about her business as if nothing unusual was happening.

  March and Omie huddled together, consoling each other as best they could as the long night bore down on them.

  In the early hours of dawn, when the sun should have been rising, it remained pitch black. The wind though was losing some of its punch. March and Omie prayed: "Dear God, please make this storm subside, so we can get a search party on the river to find Amie."
  Omie stirred the coals in the stove and filled the firebox with wood in preparation for making breakfast. She knew March would need all his strength for the trying day before him.

  It was the same in the big house. Mr. Price and Mr. Ireland had not been to bed all night. Martha had kept them supplied with coffee and sandwiches. Mrs. Sutter seemingly had no problems sleeping. Martha, too, built the fire higher in the stove in preparation for breakfast.

After a hurried meal of eggs and grits, March hurried to the main house. He asked Mr. Price if Martha could cook some cornbread and side meat for the people in the gin house. March knew they hadn't had anything to eat since noon yesterday. Mr. Price gave his consent and Martha started frying cornbread and bacon as quickly as she could.

When the food was cooked, March carried it, along with a large amount of syrup to the gin house. Those waiting there were grateful to March for the food. They wanted to know when they could leave. March replied, "As soon as the wind dies down a little more. I don't want you to go home and start fires that might burn everything down."

As soon as it was fully daylight, March had Leroy saddle his horse. He informed Mr. Price he was going to Wacissa to see if the children had gotten back; if not he would organize a search party to go down river to look for them.

The road to Wacissa was criss-crossed with downed trees. Debris littered the landscape. March was glad he was riding a horse rather than being in a wagon. He didn't think a wagon could get through on the road.

When March rode into Wacissa the winds were almost calm. People were milling about trying to assess damages done to their property. As he passed the depot, he recognized some of the people who were supposed to have gone with Amie. He hurried to them and asked, "Where are Amie and all the rest?"

"Mr. McCloud, we didn't go with the boats. We were driving the wagons to Goose Pasture to pick up the boats and people. We turned around when the storm struck and came back. We managed to get to the depot and spent the night here. We are trying to find some boats so we can start a search down river for the others."

March urged them to intensify their search for the boats and get them to the river as quickly as possible. He set off in search of one himself.

As word spread of the possible tragedy on the river, the people of Wacissa began to gather in small groups. Soon, boats began to appear and were rushed to the river and launched in preparation for the search. Crews were assigned.

When March appeared, he commandeered the nearest one and set off down river with all possible haste. Others followed soon afterward. The winds had become calm, and soon the first signs of the sun came slanting through the ragged clouds. The river looked much the same as it always did. March became hopeful that the main fury of the storm had spared it.

Periodically, they ceased paddling and drifted with the current, searching the shore for signs of survivors or wreckage. March called out numerous times hoping for some response.

Looking behind them March could see other boats crowded with rescuers, paddling furiously trying to catch up. March continued to call out as they made their way down river. If there was evidence of passage or catastrophe left by Amy and her party, the ever flowing river had erased all the signs.

The birds had returned to their normal routine of fishing and calling. Alligators and turtles were sunning themselves on the river bank and logs. They paddled on, heavy of heart.

Someone back in Wacissa had the presence of mind to prepare food for the survivors, if there were any. It was loaded aboard a boat and hurriedly sent down river.

By now, everyone knew there were possible victims somewhere down the river. More people assembled at the head of the river as the word spread.

Around noon, parents and friends of those on the outing gathered at the headwaters to learn the fate of the adventurers. Among them were the Irelands and Mr. Price.

Mrs. Ireland had insisted on coming, although she continued to vocalize her criticism toward her husband for permitting Van to go. No one paid much attention to her but Mr. Ireland. He was humiliated and discomfited in her presence.

March was exhausted from his all night vigil. Now after intense searching and rowing, his hands were blistered. His eyes felt seared from the sun's fierce rays dancing off the river's surface. He was losing heart by the minute. He reasoned with agony in his voice, "We should have found some evidence of them by now--**something**."

March slowly searched the banks, then shifted his gaze down river. His eyes were so tired he kept seeing spots on the river. There in the distance was something-- more spots he guessed.

This time the spots stayed. He stood up for a better view, and painfully said, as if in a daze, "Maybe it is a string of cypress roots in the water. No, no, it can't be. Whatever it is, it seems to be moving." March turned to the man in the rear of the boat, and said, "Look, man, straight ahead, there, near that big cypress tree, do you see anything?"

After a long pause, he received the answer he was hoping for, "I do believe you're right, Mr. March. It looks like boats to me. Several of them."

March felt weak in his knees. He sat down momentarily but came back to his feet to satisfy himself there really were boats coming. He knew it was possible it might be fishermen coming back from the Gulf with a load of fish. "Lord," he prayed silently, "let it be Amie and her friends."

After what seemed like hours, but in reality less than five minutes, the boats drew near to each other. March could see people standing and waving to him. Soon he could hear them shouting, "Boy, we sure are glad to see you!"

Then March saw a familiar face. It was Amie, she was safe! A flood of relief came over him, forcing him to sit down. Tears of joy and gratitude came to his eyes. "Thank you, Lord," he whispered.

They stopped just long enough to transfer Amie to March's boat to ease the burden on those doing the poling. Then they slowly started making their way back upstream. More and more rescue boats converged on the little flotilla. Cries of joy rang out as loved ones and friends found each other.

As the boats milled about in the middle of the river, rescuers clambered into the boats, swapping places with the tired polers. When the transfers were completed, they set off once again for home.

The storm victims were weary, almost starved, but they had survived. Soon the boat carrying provisions moved into view. When it was discovered there was food aboard, a great shout went up from the tired excursionists.

After eating, the rescued were allowed to drowse while being poled to safety. It was past midnight when the flotilla returned from the rescue mission.

Those waiting on shore heard them long before they materialized from the darkness. They began to shout from the shore to those in the boats, "Did you find anybody?"

When the answer came back, "Yes, we found all of them. They are fine," a cheer arose from shore. Sobs of joy could be heard.

And, thus ends an adventure that will long be remembered as one that almost had tragic consequences. It also hastened the end of the Irelands' visit to El Destino. Mr. Ireland was too ashamed to stay longer. Van wanted to stay, but his mother badgered him into submission. Uncle Dan assured him he was welcome to come back anytime, whether he was in residence or not. With many promises to Amie, Van sadly departed. Whatever those promises were, Amie kept them secretly in her heart.

The talk of the storm and the miraculous return of the boaters dominated all the conversations for weeks. Amie remained close to Omie and March for the next few weeks. She expressed her appreciation for life and loving parents.

March was kept busy assessing the damage to the crops. It was devastating. The buildings were damaged extensively, and they would require much repair. Thank God, no lives were lost, although one house had been blown for a considerable distance with the occupants still inside.

First thing to be done was to cut down timber to be sawed into lumber. Much materials would be needed to repair the damage done by the storm. A great stack of lumber was already cut and dried and stored for just such an occasion. It would, of course, be used to repair El Destino's damage first, and the repairs were started immediately.

The sawmill which had stood idle for long periods of time was swiftly put into operation. All hands were put to work, some felling trees, others dragging the logs to the mill to be sawed. As the lumber was cut, it was stacked pig pen style in order for the wind to circulate through the stacks and speed the drying process.

Even before they started sawing, orders were pouring in. It seemed almost everyone had suffered some damage. For more than a month, the sawmill was kept humming from first light until it was too dark to see. Still they lagged behind with the orders.

March hardly had time to say hello and goodbye to Omie. Mr. Price handled the billing and collecting, and so freed March from that exacting and time consuming job.

Most of the orders were sold on credit until crops could be sold. For those who had lost their crops completely, credit was extended on faith. Gradually, orders slowed, then ceased.

The men returned to the fields to salvage what remained of the crops. The cotton was beaten to the ground, a total loss, and not worth the effort to salvage it. It would have to be plowed under to rot over the winter.

The corn was knocked flat on the ground. A major effort was intensified to salvage as much as possible. It was the life blood of every family, eaten three times daily either in the form of bread or grits. Most meals consisted of both. The mules depended almost totally on corn. Without the mules there would be no farming activities. When the men salvaged all they could, what few grains remained, the hogs would consume.

Sweet potatoes weren't damaged and would be plentiful. This was a huge blessing because they contained much needed vitamins and were enjoyed by almost everyone.

Much of the sugar cane was blown to the ground, but like the corn it could be harvested with a lot of effort. Cane syrup ranked beside corn in importance to El Destino. It, too, was a major part of the diet. Like meal and grits it was eaten at every meal.

The peanuts had long been plowed up and stacked for drying. Soon the air will be filled with the aroma of roasting peanuts. Everyone always carried a pocket full to eat at every idle moment. Many were turned into peanut butter, a favorite of the children. The hogs would root up and eat those that remained in the ground. The storm had been a major setback for El Destino, but its inhabitants would survive.

Pork was an important source of food for the inhabitants of El Destino, and as a consequence the plantation raised a plentiful supply of hogs. A typical hog killing day proceeded as follows:

As soon as the weather turned cold, it was time to "kill hogs." The entire year's meat supply had to be processed while the weather was cold enough to keep it from spoiling. When the first frosty weather came that was judged to be the real thing, then all hands turned out for this effort.

Early on the morning of the kill, the syrup kettle was filled with water. Then a fire was lighted under the kettle and the water brought to a rolling boil.

Next, several hogs were killed. A knife was then inserted into the hog's heart, and its throat cut to release all the blood from the body. Then the hog was put into the boiling water and turned from side to side to ensure that all areas were scalded.

The hair was tested to see if it would pull out easily, and if so, the hog was quickly removed and laid on a table. Several people immediately began to remove the hair with their hands. If some hair refused to be pulled out, then a knife was used to shave it off at the base of the skin.

The hog's rear legs were then slit to reveal the hamstring. After this, a "gamble stick" was inserted so the hog could be hung upside down from a beam or from a limb. Then the hog was opened up from its throat to its rear end and the insides removed.

Next the hog was separated by sawing down the middle of the backbone. The two sides are further separated into hams, shoulder, and middling. The middling, the part between ham and shoulder, was commonly referred to as "sow belly." Sow belly was perhaps the most important part of the hog. It was fried brown for bacon, or used freely to season practically every dish eaten in the South. It was preserved in one, or two ways---either heavily salted or smoked along with the shoulders and hams.

The liver and lungs, called "lights," were saved for making a savory hash or fried fresh.

The entrails were used in several ways. Some were eaten as "chitterlings." Thoroughly washed and cleaned several times, battered and fried, they were deemed delicious. The remainder were used as casings for sausage.

The meat was ground, then seasoned with secret ingredients and forced into the casings, tied at the ends and hung over long sticks in the smokehouse. A small fire made from hickory or oak wood was placed under the sausage and kept smoldering for several days. This allowed the meat to dry and cure, thus preserving it.

As the hogs were cut up and prepared for smoking, small bits and pieces of fat, as well as lean were trimmed away. These morsels were placed in the washpot to cook. As the meat cooked, the fat was released. As it cooled it congealed into pure, white lard.

The remains were called "cracklings." When added to biscuits or cornbread, they became a real treat. Lard was the equivalent of cooking oil. It was the chief shortening in biscuit making. It was also used for greasing wagon wheels and shoes to make them soft and waterproof, and even in making soap.

Soon after hog killing time it was time to "make syrup." The routine was similar to "hog killing." All the neighbors were notified of the date and time "syrup making" would commence. Syrup making usually began early in the morning. Sugar cane was brought to the site of the mill and stored nearby. A mule was harnessed to a long, wooden arm attached to the top of the mill. The mule walked in a circle to turn the rollers. There were usually three rollers but could be only two.

Sugar cane was then fed between the rollers, and the juice was squeezed from the stalks. The stalks exited the rollers and fell to the ground. They were then thrown on a pile, called "the pummy pile." The juice ran into a barrel or sometimes a tub, then was emptied into a large iron kettle known as a "syrup kettle."

A fire was lighted under the kettle and the juice was brought to a boil. As the kettle boiled, impurities arose to the top. They were skimmed away and put into a barrel (buck barrel) to ferment. Moonshine whiskey could be made from this, or it could be left to ferment and made into beer. Only the foolhardy would imbibe this deadly witches' brew. Consequences were sure to follow--a wicked hangover and diarrhea at a minimum.

The juice was allowed to boil until the person making the syrup judged enough water had evaporated. Then the fire was quickly removed from under the kettle. The syrup was removed from the vat and stored in wooden casks (kegs). Some people preferred to use clay jugs. The jugs were sealed with a corncob for a stopper.

Children loved to play on the pummy pile. Everyone enjoyed drinking cold cane juice and were sure to take some home. Mothers and fathers caught up on all the happenings of the year, and then issued invitations to their cane grinding. This process would continue throughout the community until all had "made syrup."

After that followed peanut or corn shellings (these would be next year's seeds). Along with these events, candy would be made for the enjoyment of those participating. Taffy and peanut brittle were the favorites. The small children occupied their time playing games, such as fox and hounds, follow the leader, or spin the bottle. It was a pleasant time for all and filled the time between planting and harvesting.

At the end of the year, Mr. Price left El Destino in the capable hands of March McCloud and disappeared back into the business world. The plantation once again came alive as preparations were begun for a new season. Recovery from the devastation of 1835 was going to take a long time.

March recorded in his logbook the last day of the year, 1835:

Clear and cold. Temperature 50 degrees high, 18 degrees low. Repaired equipment today. Getting ready for spring plowing. No deaths, no sick. 1835 was a bad year, fierce storm, much damage, hope to do better in 1836.
Respectfully,
March McCloud

After her ordeal and rescue Amie spent most of her time at her home in Tallahassee. She made a half-hearted attempt to assume an active roll in the bank but soon gave it up. She attended most of the social activities and, of course, received many proposals for marriage, which she successfully evaded.

There were rumors the bank was in trouble and might fail. She was re-assured by her partners. The rumors persisted throughout 1836. Then, there was a flurry of activity to sell bonds to raise operating capital. Again, Amie was re-assured that all was well.

But all was not well. In 1837, the bank failed. Amie was ruined, wiped out along with many landowners. The entire state was affected. Even some foreign governments that had bought bonds lost their capital. Amie's house was forfeited along with the bank's assets, as well as her partners' interests.

Prince Murat lost his funds. He returned to France to seek a settlement of his inheritance. He never returned. In later years, his wife did receive his estate.

Amie became destitute, and she moved in with her parents. The glory years, it seemed, had passed. The sound of music ceased coming from the great plantation houses and those of the wealthy. The long lines of carriages waiting to deposit well-to-do guests in front of opulent homes evaporated. Many people lost their money; their property was forfeited or sold to satisfy creditors. Friendships were destroyed and families broken apart. It was the end for some, literally. They shot or hanged themselves.

Chapter 17

In the years after the great storm of 1835, Amie received letters from Van telling her of his love and promising to come as soon as he could. He was heavily involved in his family's affairs and under great pressure from his mother to conform to her wishes. She threatened to kill herself if he left home or married Amie. She was always ill and needed him. His father needed him to share the responsibility and a thousand other things. Again he promised Amie he meant to become his own boss.

He revealed to Amie his mother's objections of her when they first visited El Destino. It came as no surprise to Amie. Others had treated her the same way.

Van wrote saying, "I intend to marry you no matter what my mother says as soon as I receive my inheritance from my aunt's estate."

Amie believed him.

Amie spent most of her time riding the fine horses Mr. Price still owned. He wasn't involved with the fall of the Union Bank and so was spared. He came infrequently and stayed for brief periods. He welcomed Amie and offered her the use of the great house. Amie was appreciative but declined his generosity. She wanted a house such as the one at El Destino, but she wanted it to be her own. She would bide her time---maybe someday...

The years following the storm were good ones. El Destino prospered under the guidance of March's sure hand. Mr. Price had shown his confidence in March by raising his salary each year. For the first time, March felt secure. He and Omie had saved most of March's salary. They now had a little nest egg to see them through their twilight years. One day, when they were no longer able to work, they desired to have a place of their own.

No one in March's family had ever owned land of his own. If it was within his power, he would like to share with his family. Omie's mother died the year following her visit. Her father was barely surviving. From time to time, they sent him a few dollars.

March had asked permission from Mr. Price to have him come and live in one of the shanties. Mr. Price was quick to grant approval but warned March that he was getting along in years and couldn't guarantee anything permanent. March understood and thanked him. On those terms and as soon as Omie could get her father to agree, they would send for him.

Another year passed. Still, Van couldn't get away from his mother and the business.

Omie's father couldn't bear the thought of leaving Kansas and the grave of his wife in that lonesome place.

The plantation was running full steam. March was consumed with the activity.

The Indian War was not going well. The Indians had fled to the Everglades and couldn't be routed out. Some were hiding near Perry and the coast. They were like shadows, seen only briefly.

Mr. Price returned in 1839. He announced, "This time I intend to stay for a long while." He opened the great house, and soon he was sending out invitations to former friends. He asked Amie to make all the arrangements for him. As time passed, he became more and more dependent upon her.

He wanted Amie to move into the house and occupy the top floor. At first she refused, but as she became more and more involved in his affairs, she gave in. He asked her to do all his business correspondence, prepare his guest list, and host all his social functions. She was included in everything. When out of town guests came, he warned her of those who would snub her, and she stayed apart from them.

Mr. Price and Amie frequently rode together. He was delighted with her company. He never made improper advances toward her, nor would he allow anyone else to do so. He tried to pay Amie for the work she did for him. She refused, pointing out it was she who should pay him.

The plantation came to life again, and so did Amie. For the first time since she lost her home and money, she felt as if there might still be a future for her. She loved being the host for Mr. Price, but she felt no need to cling to the upper-class as she once had.

One day, Mr. Price went riding after lunch as he was accustomed to doing. When the hour grew late and he still had not returned, Amie became a little concerned.

Then came a knock upon the door. When she answered, there stood Leroy concern showing on his glistening face. "Miss Amie, where you reckon Marser Price is? It ain't like him to be out so late. You reckon he be all right?"

"Leroy, I'm beginning to feel concerned for him too. Maybe you better saddle a horse and go look for him."

"Yas, 'um, I 'spect I better. I's gonna go right now."

Leroy was gone only a short time when Amie heard the pound of fast approaching hoofs. She ran to the door as Leroy slid to a stop. He leaped to the ground and shouted to her, "Lawd God, Miss Amie, Marser Price is dead! I fount him a'laying in de road all covered in blood."

"Dead, you say! Leroy, where is he?"

"I fount him on de road to de sawmill, Miss Amie."

"Quick, Leroy, harness the wagon, while I get my father."

"Yas, 'um, Miss Amie, I be's fas as I can."

Amie ran to her father's house and rushed through the door calling for him. "Pa, Ma, come quick. Something has happened to Mr. Price!"

"Yore Ma's out back. What is it, Amie; what has happened to Mr. Price?"

"I don't know, Pa. He was late in returning from his ride. I sent Leroy to look for him. Leroy came back and said he had found him dead on the road to the sawmill. Come on! Leroy's hitching up the wagon."

They raced out of the house and went to the stables where Leroy was just finishing hitching the mules to the wagon. March said, "Quick, Leroy throw some of those horse blankets in the back of the wagon and get in. Amie, hurry! Get in; let's go! Where exactly is Mr. Price, Leroy?"

"He lying in de middle of de road, Marser Cloud."

"I'll drive, you show me where he is. Amie, you in yet?"

"I'm in. Let's go!"

March shouted and slapped the mules with the reins. The wagon gave a lurch as the mules took up the slack in the traces. They left at a dead run, their hooves pounding a drum beat on the hard packed sand as they headed for the mill road. When they reached the mill road, March had the mules running for all they were worth.

Leroy was hanging on with both hands, and his eyes were large and bulging. Amie was seated on the horse blankets holding on to the sides of the wagon. March kept asking Leroy where he had seen Mr. Price. "He jus' a little way now, Marser Cloud. Rat dare, Marser Cloud, rat dare in de middle of de road; see him, you see him, Marser Cloud? He daid sho nuff; ain't he, Marser Cloud?"

As March stopped the mules, he said to Leroy, "I don't know Leroy. That's what we intend to find out."

March jumped to the ground and hurried to the lump lying still on the ground. He was covered with blood, just as Leroy had said. He looked dead. Amie and Leroy, by this time were at March's side. With concern, Amie asked, "Pa, is he really dead?"

March replied, "Give me a minute."

March got down on his knees beside Mr. Price. He studied his face intently, then felt for a pulse, first on his wrist, then on his neck. He called to Mr. Price, but received no answer.

He turned to Amie and Leroy. "I cain't tell if he's alive or dead. I cain't feel any pulse. If he's breathing, it shore is faint. Leroy, pull that wagon up close, and we'll put him in."

"Yas, Suh, Marser Cloud."

"Amie, get down here with me, and let's see if we can tell where he's injured."

Amie got down beside March, and they began to look Mr. Price over to see if they could tell what had happened to him. They saw lots of blood, so there must be a wound somewhere. March gently rolled Mr. Price on to his side.

At once he could tell the wound must be somewhere on his back. When March looked closer, he could see what appeared to be a small round piece of wood sticking out of his back. At first, all March could think of was somehow he had stuck something into his back. How could such a thing happen?

March felt again for a pulse. This time he thought he detected a faint one. A weak groan came from Mr. Price. "Mr. Price, Mr. Price, this is March, are you all right? Can you hear me? Mr. Price, talk to me. We've found you. You're going to be all right. Can you hear me? Leroy, where are you? Get that wagon here. Hurry!"

"I's coming, Marser Cloud, fas as I can."

Leroy pulled the wagon close as he dared to Mr. Price. He jumped down and came alongside March. "Is he daid like I say he wuz, Marser Cloud?"

"No, he's not dead yet, Leroy. Grab hold of his feet and be careful. We're going to put him in the wagon."

Leroy held Mr. Price's feet as they lifted him into the back of the wagon onto the horse blankets. There was a low moan as they laid him down. Amie got in and sat next to him, pillowing his head in her lap. March and Leroy got into the wagon. March gently slapped the mules with the reins and called, "Get up, now!"

They started for home. March drove carefully as he could. Leroy kept looking back at Mr. Price and saying, "He sho nuff daid; ain't he, Marser Cloud?"

"Leroy, I told you already; he ain't dead, but he ain't far from it."

"Yas, Suh, Marser Cloud, dat what I say all along. I knowed he was daid de fust time I seed him."

"Leroy, get in the back with Miss Amie and help her keep him from moving. Go on, now."

"Lawd God, Marser Cloud, you ain't gonna make me tech no daid man, is you?"

"Leroy, if I have to tell you one more time he ain't dead, I'm going to stop and get a lightered knot and bust your head open; you hear me?"

"Yas, Suh, Marser Cloud, I hears you. Leroy hears you good."

As they hurried to the house, Amie kept telling Mr. Price he was going to be all right. When the wagon hit a rough place, he would cry out with a soft moan. Amie kept talking, trying to assure him he was safe.

When March stopped the wagon in front of the house, he turned and said to Leroy, "Leroy, as soon as we get Mr. Price into the house, I want you to saddle Big Red for me as quickly as you can. I'm going to ride for Doc Riley. Then, I want you to run and tell George to get some of the women and bring them to help Miss Amie."

March and Leroy carried Mr. Price to the nearest bed and put him on it. Mr. Price groaned, his eyes fluttered open for just a second. He whispered, "They shot me, March. They shot me."

"Who shot you, Mr. Price? No one shot you. You have a piece of wood in you, that's all."

"No, no, it was Indians. They shot me with an arrow."

"Indians, Mr. Price? Are you sure? We ain't seen no Indians around here."

Slowly, Mr. Price told March what had happened. He was riding when he decided to check on the gristmill. He had just ridden up when he saw smoke coming from the mill room.

He thought somehow it had caught fire. He hollered for the men who were supposed to be working there to come put the fire out. When they didn't respond to his call, he decided they might be in a shed just a short distance away.

As he turned his horse, three Indians came through the door and ran toward him. He spurred his horse, jumping away from them. He knew in a instant what was happening. The Indians had set the fire. Now they wanted to kill him, if they could catch him.

As he raced away, he was grateful he hadn't stepped from the saddle. He felt something hit him in the back. He wasn't sure what it was, but it nearly knocked him from his horse. He hung on and continued to spur for home. Soon, he knew he was seriously hurt and probably wouldn't make it to the house. He couldn't remember falling from his horse, or anything after that. "Am I hurt bad, March?"

"Mr. Price, I really don't know how bad you're hurt. I'm riding Big Red for Doc Riley. I'll be back as soon as I can. Amie and Omie will take care of you until Doc Riley gets here. You're going to be all right."

Mr. Price didn't answer. He had passed out again. Omie came rushing in and said, "March, Leroy just came and told me Mr. Price was dead, then he ran out." Then seeing Mr. Price lying on a bloody bed, Omie gasped, "March, what happened? Is he really dead?"

"No, Omie, he ain't dead, but he's seriously hurt. I'm riding for Doc Riley just as soon as Leroy brings me my horse. All I know is what Mr. Price was able to tell me just now, before he passed out. He said he was attacked by Indians at the sawmill. Apparently they set fire to it too. As soon as I leave, have George send to Tallahassee for the sheriff. Tell him what's happened and ask him to come at once. Maybe they can catch them Indians. I want him to bring along some men with guns to guard this place too. If Mr. Price's horse doesn't come in tonight, George can take some men in the morning and look for him. I'll have George post some men around the house in case those Indians decide to come here. I don't think they will though. They are probably miles away by now."

On his way to the stable, March met George and briefed him on what to do. Leroy was waiting and handed March the reins saying, "He a'raring to go, Marser Cloud."

March swung into the saddle, and before his foot was in the stirrup Big Red was almost in full stride. March let him run. He covered a mile before slowing down. As darkness descended he had to the reign the horse in. It was too dangerous to ride fast.

It took March two hours to ride to Monticello. When he got there he rode straight to Doc Riley's office. He leaped from the saddle and hurried to the doctor's door. As luck would have it, Doc Riley had just returned from delivering a baby. March quickly told him what had happened and the grave condition he believed Mr. Price to be in. "Please hurry, Doc!"

"Man, I just got back. I've been gone since yesterday. Delivered a baby over to the Tolivers. You say he's got an arrow in his back?"

"Well, I seen this piece of wood in his back. Mr. Price says they shot him. As he was riding away he felt something hit him in the back. I just reckon it must be an arrow."

"March, while I'm getting some supplies together go over to the stables, and tell Abe to saddle his best horse for me. You bring him back, and I'll be ready to go when you get here."

March mounted and rode to the stables. He told Abe what Doc Riley had said. "I guess you better saddle a fresh one for me too." Big Red was a good horse, but March didn't want to over-tax him.

Soon, Abe had two horses saddled and brought them to him. March returned to Doc Riley's office. Dr. Riley came out as soon as March called and mounted up. They set off at a trot, afraid to run the horses in the dark.

It was still dark when they reached the house. Leroy met them at the door and took the horses' reins. They hurried into the house. Dr. Riley went immediately to Mr. Price's side. He felt his pulse and took his temperature. "His pulse is very weak, and his temperature is extremely high. Both are very bad signs," Doc said.

March asked, "Can you save him, Doc?"

"I don't know, March. He's in a bad way. Now, where is that piece of wood you were telling me about?"

"It's in his back, Doc."

"All right, help me to roll him over. Be easy, now. Miss Amie, I'm going to need plenty of hot boiling water and all the clean towels you can find. Tear up some sheets and boil them for bandages."

Amie replied they had already done all those things. Doc Riley just looked at her and said, "That's fine, Amie. You didn't by chance get that arrow out; did you?"

Amie smiled and replied, "No."

When they got Mr. Price on his side, Dr. Riley said, mostly to himself, "I wonder how far that thing is in him? Sure wish we had the part that broke off."

"Doc, I heard what you said. You're in luck. Leroy found it when we loaded Mr. Price into the wagon; he didn't mention it at the time. He brought it to me later. I'll get it for you," said Amie.

She handed the broken arrow to Dr. Riley. He took it and looked it over, trying to judge how long it was originally. "March, I believe that most of the arrow is in Mr. Price. That means, unless I'm mistaken, the point is just about clear through him. That what you think?"

March took the broken arrow and studied it for a minute and then said, "I believe you're just about right in your thinking, Doc."

Dr. Riley bent down and started cutting the shirt from Mr. Price saying, "Amie, I'm ready for a pan of that hot water and a wash rag, please."

She handed them to him. He returned the rag and said, "I'm going to need an assistant. I'm nominating you. Can you do it?"

"Just tell me what to do."

Dr. Riley told Amie to clean around the wound. "When you finish, I want you to wash this spot real good on his chest." Doc pointed to the spot.

Amie looked puzzled, and Doc said to her, "That is where we are going to push that arrow out, if we are lucky." Doc then had Amie put the broken piece of arrow into a pan and boil it for a few minutes. When Amie indicated the arrow had boiled long enough, Doc poured alcohol on to the broken end that protruded from Mr. Price's back.

He said to March, "Keep Mr. Price on his side. Amie, you watch that spot on his chest and let me know if you see that arrow coming through, or a bulge in that area, okay?"

He doused the boiled arrow with alcohol and carefully fitted the broken ends together and began to push. The parts that were fitted together soon disappeared into Mr. Price's back. Amie said, "Doc, his chest is beginning to bulge."

"Fine, fine, just keep watching. When the point comes through, let me know."

Amie cried, "Here, it comes Doctor! I can see the point now."

"As soon as the wood part comes through, Amie, let me know," Dr. Riley said, as he gently continued to push.

"There it is, Doctor; I can see it now!"

Doc Riley pushed it through just a bit further then went around front to see for himself. The point was through and with a clean rag, Doc seized it and pulled the arrow from his chest. He poured alcohol on the wound then applied a compress and taped it securely. Doc returned to Mr. Price's back and pulled the other part of the arrow out.

He treated the wound with alcohol and bandaged it. Doc said, "We were lucky to know which way to push that thing. If I had tried to cut it out, we probably would have killed Mr. Price. It's very serious; may kill him yet. We'll just have to wait and see."

They made Mr. Price as comfortable as possible, while Martha cooked breakfast for them. Doc was tuckered out and fell asleep in a chair. When Martha called, Amie woke him, and for the first time in twenty-four hours he had a substantial meal. After eating Doc checked on Mr. Price.

About an hour later George rushed into the house and informed March that Mr. Price's horse had just come to the stable. March said, "George let me know when the sheriff and his men get here. In the meantime, y'all keep a sharp look-out fer them Indians. We shore don't want them to sneak up on us."

March kept his gun handy. Mr. Price's guns were loaded and standing nearby. Even so, March wished the sheriff would hurry and come.

Chapter 18

One of the men came to the door just before daylight and said he could hear the sounds of horses. March went outside as the sheriff and some of his men rode into the yard. The sheriff said, "McCloud, what's going on out here? Your man said Mr. Price has been shot by Indians and the mill burned. Is that so?"

"Sheriff, that's what Mr. Price himself said. No one else has seen anything. Doc Riley has been here most of the night caring for him. If you and your men will come in, I'll have Martha cook you some breakfast."

"We would be much obliged; it's a long ride from Tallahassee."

They came into the house glancing at the unconscious man who lay nearby. The sheriff had a brief conversation with Doc, then he and his men sat down to one of Martha's finest meals. While they ate, March filled them in as best he could.

"I'll need one of the hands to show us the way to the mill as soon as daylight comes," the sheriff said to March.

As the first peek of daylight glimmered in the sky, the sheriff and his men rode for the mill with one of the hands leading the way.

When they arrived, all that remained of both mills was the charred machinery. The buildings were burned to the ground.

The sheriff and his men dismounted and began a search for clues that might put them on the track of the Indians. There were a few tracks but none that indicated the direction of flight.

After several minutes had elapsed, someone shouted for the sheriff to come over that they had found something. When he got to where the men were standing, he saw the remains of what had once been men.

They had been scalped. When their guide saw the bodies he fainted. When he regained consciousness he got to his feet shouting: "Lawd God, Lawd God!" He ran leaving his mule behind.

The sheriff and his men milled around most of the day, but never could find in which direction the Indians escaped. After eating an early supper with March and his family, they rode for Tallahassee saying they would continue the search at a later time.

March sent George with a few men to retrieve the scalped bodies for burial. The gristmill would have to be rebuilt, and the sawmill should be too. He would decide on those details at a later time, after Mr. Price's health had been determined.

Dr. Riley stayed for two days doing everything he could for Mr. Price. He finally said, "I have done all I can for the time being." He instructed Amie how to care for him and gave her some medicine to administer. "If he gets worse, send for me, otherwise I will be back in two days." With a wave he mounted and rode away.

Amie and Omie took turns sitting with Mr. Price. His fever remained dangerously high. They constantly bathed his face and arms to keep him cool. He was delirious most of the time and had to be restrained in his bed.

Dr. Riley returned in two days as promised. He told Amie and Omie they were doing as much for Mr. Price as he could. "Continue to give him his medicine and try to keep the fever down with cold compresses. That's all we can do."

Every two days thereafter, as he promised, Dr. Riley returned to check on Mr. Price.

Days and nights ran together for Amie and Omie. One of them was always at his side. Then one day Mr. Price's fever began to drop.

Three days later it was nearly normal, and his eyes fluttered and opened for just a moment.

Shortly after that, he remained awake for longer periods. One morning his memory suddenly returned. He questioned Omie and Amie extensively about his condition. He asked, "How long have I been in bed?" Without waiting for an answer he asked, "Have they captured the Indians who shot me?" He immediately followed with, "Where is March? What are the conditions on the farm?" They answered all his questions, then sent for March.

March was beside himself with relief at Mr. Price's progress. He couldn't hold back the emotion that flowed over him as he talked with Mr. Price. Neither could Mr. Price. There was a bond between the two men that was evident to everyone in the room. Martha had come in to bring Mr. Price a cup of sassafras tea and upon observing the sentiment between them, dashed out of the room dabbing at her weeping eyes with a tea towel.

As the days passed, Mr. Price began to recover more fully. As he was still too weak to leave his bed, Amie tended his every need.

During his recovery, he slowly revealed to Amie his entire life's story. He disclosed to her all his business interests, going into great detail about their operation. Once opened, the floodgates of his life gushed forth. Amie listened but made few comments.

After more than three months had gone by, Mr. Price was able to slowly make his way around the house with some help. He came to depend upon Amie entirely. He was helpless when she wasn't there. He was pleased with Omie, too, but it was Amie who put his worries on the run.

When he grew stronger he wanted to have a party. He asked Amie to invite all his friends and hers as well. It was lavish and well attended. He seemed to enjoy himself and talked of it for several days. "We should do this more often," he said to Amie. "You need to socialize more, make new friends. Let's have another party soon. Make the arrangements."

Dr. Riley made a final visit and pronounced Mr. Price well enough for him to discontinue his visits. He wanted to take a vacation and would send his new partner, Jim Wilder, to check occasionally.

Several days later a buggy arrived at El Destino bearing the new doctor. He was a handsome man in his mid-thirties. Agile and quick of foot, he sprang from his buggy.
Amie met him at the door. He removed his hat and said, "I'm Jim; Jim Wilder. Dr. Riley asked me to look in on Mr. Price." Amie was struck with him at once.
"Please come in, we have been expecting you." He followed her to Mr. Price's room and was introduced.
After examining Mr. Price, he said that he could not find any problems and announced, "Unless you send for me, I won't be back."

Dr. Jim Wilder asked to be excused, but Mr. Price intervened saying, "Don't be in such a hurry. Stay and have lunch with us."

"That's kind of you, Mr. Price. I would be delighted."

Martha prepared a most delicious lunch for them. Mr. Price insisted that Amie stay and eat with them. Mr. Price, and Jim, as he insisted they call him, did most of the talking while Amie listened. Mr. Price was very effective in making Jim at ease. He coaxed him to reveal more of himself than he might have under normal circumstances.

Mr. Price drew Amie into the conversation, and the afternoon passed before they knew it. As Jim arose to leave, Mr. Price said, "You must come again, soon, whether I need you or not. I have enjoyed your company, and I believe that Miss Amie has too. We are having a dance Saturday next, and we would be honored if you would accept our invitation. Can we count on you?"

Jim looked at Amie, then said to Mr. Price, "That is very kind of you, Sir, I would be honored to attend. I'm new here and don't know anyone to ask to accompany me. Will it be all right if I come alone?"

"Yes, of course," said Mr. Price, looking at Amie.

When Jim had gone Amie looked at Mr. Price and asked, "What was that all about? I didn't know you were having a party."

"We are now. Why, we just needed a good excuse, and now we have one. Will you make the arrangements? And be careful of the ladies you invite this time."

Amie wondered just what Mr. Price meant by that remark, but later the answer came to her, or so she thought.

When the evening of the dance came, Amie found herself taking a bit more care with her dress. She checked the mirror several times before she was satisfied. As the guests arrived, she stood with Mr. Price to receive them. She found herself looking for one person in particular, a doctor by trade. When it looked as if Jim was not coming, Amie felt let down.

Just when the dance was getting under way, Jim came. He made his apologies to Amie and Mr. Price. He was sorry, but he had an emergency at the last minute and had to set a broken bone. Amie served him a drink and assured him all was forgiven.

When the music started, Jim was first to ask Amie for a dance. He held her firmly as they moved over the dance floor making small talk. He said he was single and had been practicing medicine for a number of years in New York City, but he had grown tired of the stuffy people there and wanted to come to a place where the people were, well, more earthy.

Amie assured Jim that none were more earthy than those he would find here. Amie found Jim asking for more and more dances. She was pleased, very pleased. Jim asked, "I did hear right, it is **Miss** Amie; isn't it?"

"Yes, you heard right. It is Miss, but I should tell you, I was married once for a short time. My husband was killed shortly after we were married. He was run over by a wagon in Tallahassee. That was a long time ago. I never remarried."

When the music stopped, Jim asked Amie to walk outside with him; "There is a beautiful moon I'd like you to see."

Jim held her hand as they strolled around the garden. It was a warm night, and the perfume from the jasmines was almost overpowering.

Finally, Jim stopped, looked into her eyes and said, "Miss Amie, if I come early next Saturday morning, would you do me the honor of riding with me? I would love to see the country. Besides, as the doctor, I need to be familiar with the area."

"I'll tell you what, Doctor," Amie replied, "I'll supply the food for a picnic, and we can ride over El Destino, if you wish."

"I do wish, and call me, Jim. I will be here early; say about nine?"

"Then, it's all settled. Shall we return to the dance?"

Amie was pleased with the way the party turned out. She thanked Mr. Price for thinking of it and told him Jim was coming back on Saturday morning.

Mr. Price looked her full in the face, then simply said, "I'm glad."

Jim came early as promised. He and Amie spent almost all day riding over the plantation, eating their lunch at the creek where the gristmill had stood. Amie told the story of its demise and of Mr. Price's wounding. She explained the mill's importance to the plantation, and she told him that her father would rebuild both the gristmill and sawmill soon.

That afternoon as they were stabling the horses, Jim held her close and kissed her for the first time. Amie didn't resist, and he kissed her again and said, "Amie, this has been one of the most wonderful days of my life. May I call on you again?"

"I would love for you to do that, Jim."

Jim became a regular visitor to El Destino after that, ostensibly to see his patient, Mr. Price. Strangely enough, even when Dr. Riley returned, Jim remained Mr. Price's doctor. Mr. Price didn't seem to mind at all.

Since his accident Mr. Price was unable to ride, even his favorite horse. He spent the majority of his time sitting at his desk pouring over reports from his vast and far flung business empire. He did, however, manage short buggy rides. Mr. Price depended more and more on Amie and March. Whatever March suggested, he usually agreed to.

March rebuilt the gristmill, then restored the sawmill. El Destino was once again a self-sustaining plantation.

Chapter 19

One day Mr. Price called March into his office and said to him, "March, on Tuesday I want you to go into Monticello and meet the train from Jacksonville. There will be two men on it. I want you to bring them to El Destino." He described the men to March and supplied their names. "While you are there, call on Mr. Thurber. I believe you know him; do you not?"

"Yes, Sir, I know him."

"Good, you will bring him along, also."

March was intrigued, of course, as to whom the visitors might be and the nature of their visit to El Destino. Oh, well, Mr. Price wasn't in the habit of discussing his business with the "Hired Help," so March put it out of his mind.

On Tuesday, March was waiting at the train station when the train rolled to a stop. March recognized the two men by the description Mr. Price had furnished him.

March introduced himself to them. When he had their luggage in the buggy, he drove to Mr. Thurber's office. He said to him, "Mr. Price directed me to bring you to El Destino. Are you ready to go?"

Mr. Thurber seemed prepared, and answered "Let me get my coat."

He came out and introduced himself to the two gentlemen in the buggy. He then took his seat, and March whipped up the horses and started for El Destino.

When they arrived at El Destino, March drove to the front of the big house to unload his charges. Mr. Price was sitting in a rocking chair on the porch. He stood and welcomed the three men. He seemed well acquainted with the gentlemen who had arrived on the train.

March drove the buggy to the stables and left it and the horses for Leroy to tend. Mr. Price told March his out-of-town guests would be staying for a day or two. Mr. Thurber would stay only for the night. March should be prepared to return him to Monticello tomorrow after lunch.

It was none of March's business, but he wondered why Mr. Price had him meet the train and drive the guests to El Destino instead of sending Leroy.

The next day after lunch, March was waiting in the buggy in front of the house as instructed. Mr. Thurber came out, slipped into the seat beside March and said he was ready to return to Monticello.

March drove him back to his office. Not a word of explanation was forthcoming from Mr. Thurber, but March expected none. Still, it was all very strange.

Two days later, March drove the other two visitors to Monticello. They boarded the train and left as mysteriously as they had arrived.

Mr. Price explained to Amie they were professional associates with business matters to discuss. Since he had not invited her presence at their meeting, she spent the time with her parents.

After their departure, everything returned to normal. Amie returned to Mr. Price's side. March resumed his everyday routine.

One day, Mr. Price said to Amie, "Amie, listen very carefully to what I have to say. Here, in my desk are two letters; they are sealed and ready for the mail. Now, in the event that something happens to me, I want you personally to immediately take these letters to Monticello and mail them. I know I can depend on you, and I want your assurance you will do this for me. Will you give me your promise?"

"Why, Mr. Price, you know I would do anything for you. Yes, of course, I will do it."

"Thank you, Amie. I don't know what I would do without you and your father. He has been a godsend to me. Amie, he has made El Destino money every year since I hired him. Why, we didn't even lose money when we had the storm. When I hired him, it was one of the best decisions I ever made. And you, you have become the daughter I always wished for."

"Why, Mr. Price, that is the nicest compliment I have ever had. My father will be pleased also."

"Then, please, convey it to your father for me. Will you?"

"I will. I want you to know also that my father is very proud to work for you. He loves El Destino with all his heart, and his admiration for you couldn't be any higher. My mother is also a great admirer of you. You have been more than generous to all of us."

Amie broke down in tears and asked, "Oh, Mr. Price, is there anything wrong?"

Mr. Price put his arms around her and said, "There, there, now Amie, I'm sorry if I upset you. There is nothing the matter. It's just that I feel it is time I told you how I feel about your family and, especially, about you."

Amie told March and Omie what Mr. Price had said. They were astonished to hear his words about them. March was aware Mr. Price had given him free rein to do almost as he pleased. He was also gratified Mr. Price depended on his judgment. Well, no sense trying to see into his mind. Just be thankful for his friendship.

Jim continued to drop by at every opportunity. When he came he always pretended to be concerned for Mr. Price. Mr. Price, in turn, would complain mildly about this or that to complete the charade. Amie would smile, enjoying the easy banter between them. Jim usually stayed for lunch, if he had the time.

Mr. Price and Amie frequently received invitations to attend parties and social functions throughout the area. Lately Mr. Price, refused to attend most of them, saying, "Amie, please, would you go and represent me? I don't think I'm up to it."

At first, she didn't think much about it, but lately she realized Mr. Price wasn't very strong after all. She began to insist he eat more and take a nap in the afternoon.

She expressed her concerns about Mr. Price to Jim. She insisted he examine him thoroughly on his next visit. Jim told her the damage Mr. Price received from the Indian arrow was probably more extensive than they knew. He added, "From what I was told by Doc Riley, Mr. Price is a lucky man to be alive. He is also fortunate you were here to nurse him. Dr. Riley gives you most of the credit for saving his life. He has told Mr. Price that many times."

On his next visit, Jim examined Mr. Price thoroughly using one pretext or another. He found him to be weaker than he expected but could find nothing seriously wrong with him. He left some medicine with Amie to give to him. "Just a tonic that will help him, I think," Jim said. With that re-assurance, Amie forgot all about Mr. Price's health.

Amie continued to hear from Van but with less and less frequency. Once, his letters so filled with promise had become vague, uncertain, and finally stopped coming. Amie couldn't decide if she was glad, or not. She realized she could never have been a real part of his family because of his mother and her friends. Amie liked his father very much. Like her, he too was often a victim. As she continued to see Jim, Van gradually faded from her mind. She found peace with the world.

    The year 1840 was well spent. March was busier than ever. He enlarged the acreage in production, and the sawmill was running almost full time. Additional workers were brought from the plantation in Georgia to augment those already at El Destino. The gristmill ran almost continually, grinding cornmeal and grits, not only for El Destino but for the surrounding area's small farmers.
    Mr. Price was more than satisfied; he gave March full authority to expand as he saw fit. This pleased March and, especially Omie. Omie said to him quite frequently, "March, I knowed you were a good provider. All you needed was a chance. I got me the best man in the whole county."

    One day, when Jim came to visit, he casually asked Mr. Price how he was feeling. To his surprise, Mr. Price complained of something specific. Jim immediately examined him.
    Later, when Jim was ready to leave, he said to Amie, "I'm afraid Mr. Price is a very sick man. From the outside he looks well enough, but on the inside I'm fearful Mr. Price may have major problems." Jim said he thought when Mr. Price was wounded the arrow passed so close to his heart that it damaged it. He was amazed problems hadn't developed before now. He also said Mr. Price could live for a long time, or might suddenly have a heart attack and die.
    Amie was shocked and saddened, "What can I do for him that will help?" she asked.
    Jim replied, "There is nothing anyone can do that I'm aware of. Just let him know you care for him and continue treating him as you usually do. Amie, I'm telling this to you in the strictest confidence. Mr. Price doesn't want to worry

anyone with his problems. He asked me not to say anything to anyone." Amie gave her word that she would keep it a secret.

Mr. Price had a wonderful family gathering at Christmas and that included March, Omie, Amie, and Jim. The workers on the plantation were not forgotten by any means and had a special Christmas, courtesy of Mr. Price.

Then, for a New Year's celebration, a grand ball was planned. Everyone from near and far was invited. Amie, as usual, was the hostess and the center of attention. Mr. Price sat beaming at her, introducing her at every opportunity.

Before the ball ended, he informed Amie, "I'm feeling tired. I believe I will go to my room." Amie assisted him to his quarters. She was worried and wanted to sit with him. He shooed her out insisting he was all right. "Go back to your friends and have fun. I'm just tired. I'll be just fine in the morning." Amie kissed his cheek, and then she returned to the festivities.

When the last guest departed, Amie returned to Mr. Price's room. She peeped inside, hoping he might still be awake. He appeared to be asleep. She closed his door and went to her own room and went to bed.

Amie was awakened from a sound sleep by a terrible scream. They continued, accompanied by loud footsteps rapidly approaching her room. Her door burst open, Martha stood there, eyes wide, mouth working. "Come quick, Miss Amie, sompin sho nuff wrong wif Marser Price! He won't wake up."

Amie's feet hit the floor and without stopping, she raced to Mr. Price's room. She called to him, "Mr. Price, Mr. Price, are you all right?"

She could see at once he wasn't all right. He was still. When she touched him, he was cold. She knew at once he was dead. What must she do?

Her senses failed her. She sat on the bed next to him trying to gather her wits. Martha stood in the doorway nervously wringing her hands. "What de matter wid him, Miss Amie? Is he daid?"

"Yes, Martha, he's dead. Go get my father."

Martha left on the run. Amie could hear her hollering for one of the girls who helped in the kitchen, "Child, you go find Marser March. Tell him Marser Price is daid."

Amie heard running footsteps, then the sound of the door slamming as the girl hurried to find March.

March came into the room. Amie was still sitting beside Mr. Price. One look told March he knew what he had just heard was true. He took Amie's hands and asked, "When did you find him?"

"Martha found him when she came to wake him for breakfast, only a few minutes ago."

"He's dead?"

"Yes, Pa, he's dead. He must have died just after I left him last night."

"Was he all right when you left him?"

"I came back to his room, hoping he was awake so we could talk. When I looked in, I thought he was asleep. I closed his door and went to bed."

March said, "First thing we got to do is let somebody know. The sheriff, I guess. I'll send Leroy."

"No, wait, Pa. Mr. Price told me what to do if anything should happen to him."

"What did he tell you to do?"

"Come down to the office with me, and I'll show you."

Amie pulled the bed sheet over Mr. Price, then she and March went down to the office. Amie opened one of the desk drawers and removed several letters. There was also a sheet of paper containing several names.

She turned to March and said, "Mr. Price said the first thing I must do is mail these letters. When you send Leroy to town, have him give them to the postmaster. Tell Leroy to tell him they must be on the noon train. Those were Mr. Price's instructions." Amy continued, "Later today I'll contact by telegraph those whose names are listed on this paper. Pa, after you get Leroy on his way to the post office bring Ma, and let's talk."

March sent for Leroy and told him Mr. Price was dead. "I want you to saddle a horse right away. Then come back and see me. I have some important things for you to do in Monticello."

"Yas, Suh, Marser Cloud, I's on de way."

When Leroy was ready to go, March gave him the letters and explained what he was to do with them. He made Leroy repeat his instructions, making sure he understood them and the urgency of his mission. "I'll skin you alive if those letters don't get on the train."

"Marser Cloud, you knows you can count on Leroy to do zackly what you say." With that he was away, dirt flying from the hoofs of his horse.

March went and got Omie, then they went to Amie's room. She was dressed when they arrived. Amie told them Martha was making breakfast for her. "Pa, have you and Ma eaten yet?"

"No, we ain't."

Amie called to Martha and told her to make breakfast for them all. While they waited in the dining room, they discussed Mr. Price's death and what was to be done. Martha brought ham and eggs and a pot of coffee, then went back for biscuits. While they ate they talked about the kindness Mr. Price had shown them. Tears welled up in their eyes. They knew a friend had passed away. Now their future was uncertain.

When they finished breakfast, March and Omie followed Amie back to the office. She told them of her conversation with Mr. Price concerning what to do if something happened to him. "Pa, in one of the envelopes he left instructions for his burial. He wants to be buried here at El Destino. He even made a map showing exactly where he wants his grave dug. Here, read it."

March read the letter. It was signed and notarized with the names of all three men March had brought from Monticello. He then realized why they were here. "They must have been his lawyers," March said. "Mr. Thurber is a lawyer, and I bet the other two were also. So, that was why they came."

"What, who, came for what, Pa?"

"Those men I brought from Monticello that time, remember? They must have been Mr. Price's lawyers. They came to make his will."

"Pa, I never saw a will, and Mr. Price never said anything about one."

"I spect those men carried it back with them to New York."

"Pa, reckon what this means for us?"

"Amie, I shore wish I knew, but I don't. We'll just have to wait and see."

"I sure hope you don't lose your job, Pa."

"Well, that's out of our hands. If it's left up to those sisters and aunt that were here one time, we'll have to go. I'm shore of that. They don't want no truck with the "Hired Help."

"Especially me, Pa."

"Amie, what does it say about his funeral?"

"I don't know, Pa. Let's see if I can find out anything."

Amie carefully read the instructions Mr. Price had left for her. She was to notify Mr. Thurber in Monticello of his death and give him the list of people to be notified. He would make all the arrangements and manage the details. Amie said, "If I had known this, I could have sent it with Leroy. Well, I need a ride anyway. Pa, I'm going into Monticello and notify Mr. Thurber. I expect he'll send the undertaker today; don't you?"

"Yes, something needs to be done soon. I'll saddle yore horse."

When March left, Amie dressed hurriedly for riding. She gathered up the papers to be delivered to Mr. Thurber, then she and Omie walked to the stables. March had her mount ready.

She mounted and rode quickly away. She savored the ride in spite of the gravity of the moment. "It may well be my last ride on a horse belonging to El Destino," she thought.

When she got to town, she sought out Mr. Thurber at once.

She explained her mission to him. He informed her he knew exactly what was required. "I'll handle all the details from now on. If you will excuse me, Miss Amie, I must find the undertaker. I will send him at once to El Destino. You may expect me early tomorrow with the details for the funeral."

"Well, it looks as if the McClouds are out of the picture from now on," Amie thought to herself.

Immediately upon leaving Mr. Thurber's office, she went to see Jim. She wanted him to know what was happening. He was not surprised. He extended his sympathy to her and her family. He said, "If you can wait for a few minutes until I see one more patient, I will accompany you home."

"Jim, if you don't mind, I would rather be alone for a while."

"Then I'll come tomorrow, if it's all right?" inquired Jim.

"Yes, please do." With her duties settled, Amie rode for home, contemplating the future and circumstances, "Home? Whose home? Probably not my home for long."

Not long after Amie returned home, the undertaker and his wife rattled to a stop in front of the house. They stepped down and said, "Howdy, Miss Amie, reckon you know who I am. This is my wife, come to help with Mr. Price. I'm right sorry about Mr. Price, a fine man. If you will show us where he is, we'll get started. We might need a few things."

"I'll tell Martha. She will supply whatever you require. Has Mr. Thurber told you when the funeral will be?"

"Well, no, not exactly, but we have plenty of time with the weather cold like it is."

After the undertaker finished, he said to Amie, "We are through for now. He is laid out on the bed for the time being. There will be a wagon coming before night with a coffin for him. They were working on it at the blacksmith shop when I left. When it comes I spect y'all ought to put him in it right away. I spect folks will be coming before dark to pay their respects. The news is spreading fast."

Amie thanked him, and he drove away. She turned to Martha, "Martha, I suppose we are in for a lot of visitors. You had better start making something for them to eat. I guess there will be a wake too."

"Yas, 'um, Miss Amie, I spect so. I's gonna need some more hep in de kitchen."

"Martha, you pick them out, and let George know."

"Yas, 'um, I's gonna need to get in de storehouse, too."

"Here are the keys. Take what you need; keep the door locked."

"Yas, 'um."

The wagon arrived with the coffin late in the afternoon. It was brought into the house and placed in the great ballroom on sawhorses. Mr. Price was then placed into the finely crafted box for viewing.

Along toward dark, folks started coming. You could see the lantern lights winking as the vehicles slowly made their way between the huge oaks that lined the driveway. Some came in plain wagons, some in fancy rigs, and some on horseback. Most had never been to El Destino. This was their opportunity to see the great estate.

Amie and her family welcomed each one and accepted their condolences on behalf of Mr. Price's family. Martha had prepared cakes and pies, along with plenty of coffee.

Some stayed for a brief time only, then left. Others stayed throughout the night. They all made numerous trips by Mr. Price's coffin to look at the former owner of El Destino. They could be heard saying what a nice man he had been.

Finally, at dawn, the mourners were gone. Amie and her family were exhausted. They gratefully slipped into bed to rest before the next onslaught.

Just before noon Mr. Thurber came. Martha woke Amie, then went in search of March. Mr. Thurber explained to them that Mr. Price had engaged him to make all the arrangements for his funeral, if it became necessary and that he had notified by telegraph all those on the list. They were told the funeral would be in five days at three o'clock in the afternoon. "What a wonderful device the telegraph is," Mr. Thurber said. "Why, in just a few minutes you can send a message and receive a reply from nearly any place in the United States. Soon we'll be connected to Europe. We will be able to send messages back and forth. Isn't that amazing?"

March agreed that was amazing indeed. He secretly thought to himself, "You pompous oaf!"

Mr. Thurber said to March, "Mr. Price's instructions to me were to inform you that, until you hear from Mr. Price's lawyers, you are in complete control of El Destino and its operations."

March said, "What does that mean?"

"It means that whatever you say is final. Just as if you were Mr. Price himself. I have sent letters to all of El Destino's suppliers informing them you have full authority to purchase any and all supplies you deem necessary. They will be paid for fully and promptly by funds available through my office." March was quite surprised to hear that.

March then asked Mr. Thurber if he knew what was to happen to him and to El Destino. "No, I do not. You will receive the answer in due course from the other lawyers, I'm sure."

Mr. Thurber spent several hours with March and Amie answering their questions as best he could. "I will be back on the day of the funeral. If I can be of help before then please send for me." He then left for Monticello.

March said to Amie, "Mr. Price sure had everything planned for his final departure. Didn't he?"

"Yes, Pa, he was a thorough man."

Until the day of the funeral, people continued coming to pay their respects and to gaze upon the former owner lying in state in an elaborately furnished house like a grand potentate.

When Martha ran low on supplies, Amie sent the wagon to town for more. The stove never cooled. Martha made stacks of sandwiches, gallons of coffee, and pies and cakes by the score.

March and Amie were constantly busy receiving guests and answering their questions as diplomatically as possible. They rarely went to bed before dawn.

Chapter 20

On the day of the funeral all work was suspended in the fields. Just the chores necessary to ensure the health of the livestock was done. The slaves would attend the funeral but at a distance. Amie wanted to have them in close, but March didn't think that a good idea. There was too much ill will about the slave question already.

Early on the morning of the funeral dignitaries began to arrive, some on horseback but most in splendid carriages drawn by matched horses. Among those attending were the Territorial Governor and his Cabinet along with many Representatives, Catherine Daingerfield Willis Murat, and most owners of the other plantations. There were judges, bankers, and lawyers, some from far away and some from Monticello and Tallahassee.

When family members arrived they were quartered in the big house, along with close personal friends. Mr. Price's two sisters, Mrs. Ireland and Mrs. Sutter, and his aunt were there. Van was there too.

Why wasn't Amie pleased to see Van? She welcomed him and his mother, and Mrs. Sutter as best she could, the aunt also. They acknowledged her with just a curt nod. Well, she owed it to Mr. Price to be nice to them. After the funeral she probably would never see them again. Van signaled that he wished to speak to her, but she was just too busy, and she just smiled at him.

Later, Van expressed his pleasure at seeing her. Amie asked why he had stopped writing and why had he not come as he promised?

He gave a lame excuse blaming his mother. He said, "Soon I will be free. I want to resume our friendship." Amie didn't ask what she was supposed to do in the meantime.

Martha outdid herself. The dining table was filled to capacity. Numerous roasts of pork and beef, a dozen or more chickens prepared in various ways; such as fried, baked, and stewed and all swimming in gallons of Martha's delicious brown flour gravy. Scrumptious dishes of sweet potatoes decked the table in every conceivable form: baked, candied, and souffled. Desserts included an array of fancy pies and cakes.

Martha and her crew had worked around the clock to keep the guests fed. The wagon rumbled back and forth to Monticello replenishing supplies. Mr. Price would have been proud.

At noon on the day of the funeral, Amie announced lunch was being served. The huge dining room was filled to capacity with senior dignitaries and family members. Those remaining, and there were many, would have to wait. They would be served along with those of lesser standing.

Some were hurt because they were unable to sit with the dignitaries; others were glad because of it. Those attending out of curiosity brought their own food, spreading it under the great oaks growing in the yard.

Then it was time for the funeral itself. George and his men had dug and prepared the grave earlier, just where Mr. Price wanted it. He had chosen a spot under the largest oak on El Destino. It grew on a shallow incline near the great house.

Mrs. Ireland grumbled at her brother's lack of sense. "Why would he want to be buried among these heathen, so far from his kin?" she lamented. Amie could barely remain civil in the face of such a put down. Because Mr. Price had been her friend, she bit her tongue.

March and Amie led the procession to the grave. There a minister from Pensacola, summoned especially for the occasion, presided over the service.

At the end of the funeral proceedings, Mr. Price was lowered, amidst sobs and tears, into his final resting place.

As the crowd dispersed, Amie stood beside Mrs. Ireland and received condolences, most of them directed toward Amie. Mrs. Ireland was heard to mumble, "That hussy must think she owns this place. I will show her what happens to the "Hired Help" when they get too big for their britches."

When it was finally over, Amie and March almost collapsed. They were utterly exhausted, along with Martha and her crew. It had been a nightmare, and they desperately needed rest.

Amie glanced behind her and saw Mrs. Ireland coming toward them. Amie could see blood in her eyes. She nudged March and said, "Here comes trouble. I think I'm about to get my come-uppance."

Without hesitating, Mrs. Ireland lit into Amie and March. "Who do you think you are?" she demanded. "You act like you own this plantation and Mr. Price was your kin. You both are fired as of this very minute, and I want you off this place before dark!"

They were stunned. They knew where they stood with her and had made an effort not to antagonize her. Now she was going to discharge them and throw them out? And at night at that! Amie was aghast and said to March, "Pa, can she do that?"

Mrs. Ireland broke in, mimicking Amie, "Pa, can she do that? You better believe I can. And I will. Get your things and leave El Destino, and I mean right now!"

Van was standing nearby but remained quiet, not daring to interfere. Without any doubt and instantly, Amie knew the last flicker of flame that had once flared between them had finally been extinguished.

Standing together beside the wall were Mr. Price's lawyers. They heard what Mrs. Ireland said to Amy and March. One of them approached her and said, "May I please speak with you privately?" She was still raging and told him off too.

He then said to her, "Mrs. Ireland, I'm Mr. Price's friend, as well as his attorney. He has made specific documents dictating precisely what is to happen to his estate. If you would allow me to say so, this is not the proper time to interfere. Please drop your demands against Mr. McCloud until we can have an official meeting. At that time, these matters can be put to rest. Until then, please I beg of you, let Mr. McCloud continue as he has been instructed in Mr. Price's will."

"Are you saying I can't fire that man and make him take that girl with him?"

"Mrs. Ireland, Mr. McCloud has been instructed by your late brother to perform certain functions here. I'm sure you would want to honor his last wish. But to answer your question, no, Ma'am, you can't fire Mr. McCloud, nor do you have authority to do anything else here. For the present, Mr. McCloud has complete authority to run this place as he sees fit. That includes deciding who stays and who goes. I'm afraid that includes you."

"Well, Mr. Lawyer, I'm still a major stockholder in all of my brother's business enterprises. I shall see my lawyer. We will see who has the final word."

"Mrs. Ireland, that's a wise decision. Please, do consult with your lawyer as soon as possible. I sincerely hope you will follow his advice."

During the entire exchange, March and Amie were wide eyed with utter surprise etched on their faces. They couldn't believe their ears.

They were speechless when the lawyer turned to March and said, "Mr. McCloud, I'm sorry you and your daughter had to be put through such humiliation. Will you please accept my most humble apology? In due time, you and your daughter will be notified of a meeting to be held in New York City. You and Miss Amie will be required to attend. At that time, final decisions are to be made known regarding Mr. Price's wishes pertaining to his estate. You will be sent tickets, your wife included, if she desires to come. Your expenses will be paid as well. Until you have further correspondence from me, please feel assured that you, and you alone, make all decisions regarding El Destino."

"Well, I thank you, Sir, but I'm mighty puzzled."

"I expect you are, Mr. McCloud; I expect you are."

The next morning March announced, "All work for the next two days will be suspended, except for feeding the livestock." Then utterly exhausted, he went to bed.

Much later that day Amie bid Van, Mrs. Ireland, and Mrs. Sutter a cheery "Good-bye. Hope to see you soon." Amie in turn received a haughty look from the ladies, and with a toss of their heads, they turned their perceived "Blue Noses" skyward, marched away to their carriage with Van following along like a puppy.

After two days of well deserved rest, El Destino returned to normal. Work for the spring planting was renewed with a zeal. The blacksmith was kept busy shoeing the mules and refurbishing their harnesses. Plows and hoes were sharpened to ensure they would cut the sod properly. Seeds were readied for sowing.

For everyone at El Destino, except March, life returned to normal. There remained a dread hanging over him. He didn't talk about it, but he wondered what the future held for Omie and him. How much longer would he have a job and a place to live? What about Amie? What would happen to her? Why was their presence required in New York City? He wouldn't give a red cent for his chances of staying on as overseer. Not with that sister of Mr. Price raging as she did. There was nothing to do but see it through. In the meantime, he meant to keep on the look-out for another job. All these things played on his mind as he went about the business of making a crop. Whose crop would it be anyway?

George came to him seeking assurance for himself and the other slaves. "Marser March, what gonna happen to us? Is we gonna be sold and bust up our family? Is you gonna stay here? Us sho hope so. Us hope us gonna stay too. Is der anything you can tell us?"

March did his best to re-assure George. He decided the truth was what George needed to hear most. "George, I'm just as much in the dark as you are. I just don't know what will happen to El Destino. I don't know what is going to happen to me, or you, or anything else. All I know is that we are to continue on until I hear from Mr. Price's lawyers. George, that's the truth. You tell that to everyone."

Three weeks later a letter arrived for March and Amie. In it were train tickets for three to New York City along with three hundred dollars in cash for expenses. A meeting had been set for two weeks later. Their presence was requested. When March told Omie about it she said, "March, you and Amie go, I cain't fit in like y'all can. I'd feel better staying at home."

When March told Amie what Omie said, Amie went to her and begged her to go. "If you don't fit in Ma, then Pa and I don't fit in either. I don't know why they want us there, but it must have been Mr. Price's idea. Ma, he was our friend. He would want you to go."

"Amie, I shore would like to see New York City. I probably won't never get another chance, so I have changed my mind. I'm a'going."

March made arrangements for the overseer at Chemonie Plantation to look in at El Destino every three or four days until he got back. George would be in charge, unless there was a problem he couldn't handle.

There had been very little trouble with the slaves since March had been there. There was a couple of runaways, but they were quickly found in Tallahassee's French Town and brought back. He felt comfortable everything would be all right until he returned.

On the appointed day, March, Omie, and Amie boarded the train in Monticello and headed for New York City to learn their fate.

When they arrived in New York City, they were met and booked into one of the best hotels. They would be picked up the next day and driven to the meeting. March could only shake his head in disbelief at all the attention they were receiving. He said, "I guess this is our going away present."

Next day, promptly at the appointed time, there was a coach waiting for them in front of the hotel. They were driven to a large office building with the name **"PRICE"** emblazoned above the door.

They were met and ushered into a huge room. It contained a magnificent table surrounded by more than two dozen chairs. "The man called it the "boardroom;" Omie said, "I don't know what a boardroom is, but a heap of folks could set and eat at that table."

Amie and March laughed but had to agree a heap of folks could indeed eat at that table.

Soon others began to gather. Some of them introduced themselves, but most took a seat and were quiet. The last persons to enter were Mrs. Ireland, Van, and Mrs. Sutter.

They ignored March and his family, taking their seats as far away as possible. This didn't go unnoticed by the rest of those assembled. Van was the only one to acknowledge them. He did so with a weak and sheepish gesture of his hand. The others in the room looked at March and his family, then in succession to Mrs. Sutter, Mrs. Ireland, and Van. They wondered what was going on but said nothing.

The lawyer who had defended March from Mrs. Ireland came into the boardroom. He welcomed March and his family, then took a seat. Mr. Thurber from Monticello arrived last. March and Amie were surprised to see him. He acknowledged their presence, this time with a lot more familiarity than he had shown before.

Mr. Price's lawyer rose and called the meeting to order. After introducing March and his family, he said, "Ladies and gentlemen, you know, of course, why we are here. It is to read the final will and testament of the late, Mr. Dan Price. If there are no objections, we will proceed."

He proceeded to read the long list of "whereas" this and "whereas" that and "therefore" this and "therefore" that. Finally he came to the part in which Mr. Price was bequeathing thus and so--to so and so.

He looked at March and said, "Mr. McCloud, you will be interested in this part of Mr. Price's will, I'm sure."

March thought to himself, "Here it comes. I'm going to be fired, and old Lady Ireland will gloat over me."

Continuing on, Mr. Price's lawyer said, "Mr. McCloud, Mr. Price bequeaths to you in gratitude for service rendered a sum of ten thousand dollars."

There was a wail from Mrs. Ireland as she screeched, "Why would he do a thing like that?"

"Please, if I may be allowed to continue," said Mr. Price's lawyer. "Furthermore, I consider Mr. McCloud and his family equal to my own. March, enjoy your retirement years, and when you ride Big Red, think of me."

"He won't be riding Big Red for long. If this meeting is over, let's get out of here; the air is bad," Mrs. Ireland said, looking at March and Amie.

Mr. Price's lawyer hushed her saying, "There is one more item to cover, and that will conclude the reading of the will. It states:

I, Dan Price, being of sound mind do hereby bequeath to my dearest friend and to my adopted daughter in wish only, Amie McCloud Weston the residue of my estate to have and to hold forever."

Mrs. Ireland fainted! Mrs. Sutter, with a whine, collapsed beside her. March was dazed, unsure if he had heard right or not. There was pandemonium amongst those in attendance.

Some were trying to revive Mrs. Ireland, while others attended Mrs. Sutter. Omie had been hugging March but turned him loose in favor of Amie, who sat open mouthed. Van stared at Amie in disbelief.

When some semblance of order had been restored, Mr. Price's lawyer turned to Mr. Thurber and asked, "Mr. Thurber, can you affirm that this last will and testament of Mr. Dan Price was made by him?"

Mr. Thurber replied, "I can and do."

"Was it made freely by Mr. Price, and is it your judgment that Mr. Price was sane at the time of its making?"

Mr. Thurber stood and said, "I was present when this will was taken. I have never seen a more sane man than Mr. Price was at that time. You will find my Notary Seal affixed to the original document and my signature indicating I was present and witnessed the signatures of my two colleagues." With that he sat down.

Mr. Price's lawyer concluded by saying, "Ladies and gentlemen, you may examine this document. You will find it has been properly drawn and executed. Copies will be furnished to each of you. One more thing and this meeting will adjourn. By virtue of the fact Mr. Price was the majority stockholder he was also Chairman of the Board. Mrs. Amie McCloud Weston is now the majority stockholder; therefore, she is the new Chairwoman of the Board. I think a round of applause is in order for her. Could we applaud Mrs. Weston?" After a polite applause, he then turned to her and said, "Madam Chairwoman, would you care to address your partners and stockholders?"

Amie struggled to her feet, her mind in a muddle and gently said, "I came here today thinking we, rather that my father, was to be relieved of the job he has held and loved for the past eighteen or nineteen years. I was overwhelmed when Mr. Price recognized my father's work and awarded him ten thousand dollars. But now--now, my mind refuses to believe Mr. Price has bestowed on me such an honor. For a long time he has called me his daughter, and I called him my second father. Mr. Price, almost to the end, kept his life a very private matter. I never--never had a hint, nor had it ever crossed my mind I would find myself in this position today. At this time I'm in no condition to fully comprehend what has happened."

The meeting was adjourned amid turmoil. Some members were happy, some left in shock and dismay.

The attorneys asked Amie to meet with them to conclude the remainder of their business. Omie and March returned to the hotel.

For several hours, Amie listened to Mr. Price's lawyers. Her head was spinning. "I must have more time. It's more than I can comprehend just now. I will meet with you again in a few days, but please excuse me today," she tiredly said to them.

When she returned to the hotel she explained to March and Omie that she would have to stay for a while longer in New York City. Many decisions had to be made concerning all the enterprises that had fallen to her. She still couldn't quite believe it had happened. They took their evening meal in Amie's room, talking long into the night.

It was decided that March and Omie would return to El Destino immediately to see to its welfare and convey the good news to the work hands. Amie would stay and attend to business. Amie said to her mother, "Ma, before you leave New York City, write to Grandpa and tell him we'll be coming for him. I want him to live at El Destino for the rest of his life."

"Oh, Amie, this is the happiest day of my life. I shore wish Ma could have lived to come to El Destino."

Amie turned to March and said, "Pa, I want you to get in touch with all your family; I want them to come to El Destino too."

March said with tears in his eyes, "Amie, there ain't nothing in the world I would rather do than have my family around me. I'll start writing as soon as I get home."

Amie was left alone in New York City with the awesome burden of trying to understand what she now was responsible for. The first day she met with the lawyers all day as they tried to lay out a picture for her she could understand. "Miss Amie, Mr. Price was a very rich man; he had his fingers in many pies. It is a vast and complex enterprise. If you choose, you may in time master the complexity of it. If you desire you may continue to depend, as Mr. Price did, on the managers he has in place. Whatever way you elect, my firm and I want to continue to serve you as we did Mr. Price. I hope you will consider us. If you say yes, I can assure you, we'll stand with you in all matters. We will always have your best interest foremost in our minds. Please take a few days, relax and enjoy New York City. When you have arrived at your decision, please let us know," the senior attorney said.

"Thank you, I will do just as you suggest. I have many friends here. I will contact some of them."

Chapter 21

That evening, Van called on Amie at her hotel. He said he had come to ask for forgiveness. He blamed his mother for keeping him from coming to Amie as he had promised. He wanted to make a fresh start. Wouldn't she please forget the past? He begged Amie, "Please, will you come to dinner with me, and let's discuss it?"

Amie surmised to herself that his mother had sent him. She replied, "No, Van, I spent a long time waiting for you to come to me. I'm over you now and have been for a long time. There are others in my life. Please don't call again."

Two days later, she received a note from Mrs. Ireland saying she was sorry and asking Amie's forgiveness. It also stated, "I have misjudged you, and I want to be your friend."

The following day, she received the same kind of note from Mrs. Sutter. Amie ignored them both, thinking, "Now that I'm the Chair of the Board you want to be my friend. If I wasn't the Chair, nothing would have changed."

Amie sent notes to some of her friends announcing that she was in town and would like to see them.

Fortunately, these were true friends who were interested in her for herself, very unlike Mrs. Ireland and Mrs. Sutter.

    Amie relaxed for a few days, then met with her lawyers again. She asked them to continue providing her with the same expertise she was sure they had provided for Mr. Price. They were pleased to accept. For several days they walked her through every phase of her new business. She was introduced to all the head administrators.
    Mr. Ireland was among them. He came to her in a moment of privacy. He gave her a warm welcome and congratulated her on her windfall. He said to her, "Amie, I hope what happened between you and my wife and son will not color or cloud our friendship. I never approved of the shabby treatment you received from them. I apologize for not being the man I should have been. In that respect, I'm just as guilty as they are. From this time on, I intend to re-establish control over my house. You have every reason to have nothing to do with me, and I wouldn't blame you. If you feel like doing that, I shall take it like a man. Amie, I'm not crawling because I fear you and what you might do to me. I truly mean what I say. If you believe me and can find it in your heart to forgive me, please do so. If you can't, I will understand."
    Amie responded, "Mr. Ireland, I liked you from the start. I have always known you disapproved of their rude behavior. Now that you have come to me and said the things you have, I like you even better." With that she put her arms around him and said, "I can't forgive you, because you aren't guilty. I hope we'll always be friends."

    Two days later, she asked Mr. Ireland to please come to her office. She said to him, "On recommendation of my attorneys and because you were Mr. Price's close associate and my friend, I want you to be the acting Chairman of the Board."

He looked at her for the longest time. His face clearly showing disbelief. He turned and walked out of her office.

A few seconds later he came back. Amie said, "I'm sorry, I thought you would be pleased."

"Amie, I was so overcome I didn't want you to see me cry. You are so much bigger than I ever imagined. I have never dealt with anyone like you. I don't have words to express my gratitude to you. You have restored my faith in people and my manhood at the same time."

"Good, I thought at first I had insulted you. There is one other thing, I hope you won't think less of me for it. I can't and won't have any association with your wife or son. You, however, will always be welcome at El Destino."

"Thank you for the invitation. Sometime I would like to come for a visit."

Amie turned over the operations of Price Enterprises to Mr. Ireland, then headed for home. News of her inheritance proceeded her. Even before March and Omie arrived back home word had gotten out.

As soon as she stepped down from the train in Monticello, Mr. Thurber was there to welcome her home. He was all smiles and wanted to know if there was anything he might do for her, "Just anything, Miss Amie. You just let me know."

"Thank you, Mr. Thurber, I will be sure to remember."

Leroy was waiting with the buggy. He had a grin a mile wide on his face. "Lawd, Lawd, Miss Amie, we sho is glad to see you is back. Us thought you might jus' stay in New York and not never come back. Marser Cloud done told all us dat you de new owner and, Miss Amie, us is sho glad."

"Leroy, you just don't know how glad I am to be back. Let's go home."

"Leroy sho gonna get you dere quick, Miss Amie; you jus' hold on."

"Wait, Leroy, take me by the mercantile store first."

"I sho nuff will, Miss Amie."

Leroy drove Amie to the store and waited beside the buggy while she went inside. Amie spoke to the owner and said, "I wish to purchase some tobacco and snuff."

"How much you want, Miss Amie?"

"Well, let's see. How many plugs in a case?"

"There are forty-eight, Miss Amie."

"I want to purchase four cases and mix it up between Brown Mule and Spark Plug. I'll need some snuff too, oh say, about two hundred boxes and divide it among Butter Cup, Railroad, Sweet Dental, and Three Thistles. Now, for some smoking tobacco, two hundred cans will do for a start. Half of it Prince Albert and half Hi Plane will be fine."

"My, my, Miss Amie, somebody's a'gonna do a lot of spitting."

"They certainly are. From time to time I will be sending for more. Just prepare and send the same order, unless I say differently."

"Yes, Ma'am, Miss Amie. I shore thank you fer the order."

When Leroy saw all the tobacco and snuff Miss Amie had ordered he said, "Lawd, have mercy, Miss Amie. I ain't never seen dis much in my whole lifetime. What you gonna do wid it?"

"Leroy, from now on, I don't mean for us to run short of anything at El Destino. Help yourself to some."

"You means I gets to keep it, Miss Amie?"

"I do, and when you chew that one up, you can have another."

"Miss Amie, us sho is glad to have you back. I wants one of dem Brown Mules."

When Amie arrived at El Destino, March and Omie were waiting for her. Amie ran to their waiting arms. They all broke down in tears. Amie said to them, "Ma, Pa, this has sure been something; hasn't it?"

They agreed. They were still wondering if all that had happened was real or a dream. Omie said, "March and me talk about hit every day, and we still cain't believe it."

Amie said, "Did you do as I asked? Have you sent letters to Grandpa, Ma? Pa, what about you? Have you written your brothers and sisters?"

"Well, I wrote Pa like you said. I told him we were coming fer him just as soon as you got back from New York City. Yore Pa said hit wouldn't be right for you to put up all his folks. He said he would help them with his money."

"Oh, Pa, I got more money than I can ever use. I want us all to be together. We have been poor long enough. I got it free, and we can give some to others now. Write them, Pa. No wait, wait. I have a better idea. Let's just go and get them in person. Just as soon as we get back from Kansas."

March said with a wistful look, "They shore will be surprised; won't they? I just wish Pa and Ma could have lived to see it."

Amie and her mother left at the end of the week for Kansas. This time they went straight through without stopping. When they got to Omie's Pa's house, it looked empty and forlorn. Weeds had grown up around it. It was bare. No animals, nothing. "Do you reckon he moved, Ma?"

"Honey, I just don't know. I got a powerful bad feeling something is terribly wrong."

They went to the nearest neighbors and asked if they knew what had happened to him. The man who answered the door was shocked, and said, "You the folks that were a'coming fer him?"

"Yes," Amie replied, "He's my Grandpa."

"Lord, Child, didn't y'all get my letter? I wrote y'all as soon as I found out you were a'coming. I shore am sorry to tell you, but yore Grandpa died about two weeks ago."

Omie wilted and sat down on the porch. Amie was stricken and sat beside her. Finally Omie said, "We never got yore letter. I guess we passed it som'mers on the way here."

He gave them the details of his death. "He came over one day to visit fer a spell. He had a letter with him. He told me he had finally decided to go to Florida and live with his daughter. He seemed to be real excited. He stayed, and we visited fer quite a spell talking 'bout hard times and all that sort of stuff, and then he left. I didn't see him fer a day or two, so I went to check on him. I found him dead. That's when I looked about and found yore address and sent a letter to you. We didn't know what to do, so we buried him out back beside his wife. I reckon that was what he would have wanted. I'm shore sorry we couldn't do better by him, but things are pure hard out here fer us. I will tell you one thing about him. If hit hadn't been fer him, we would have lost our place. He let me have fifteen dollars to pay on my mortgage. I shore wish I had hit to give to you, but I'm back in the same fix again. We shore do miss him. We been friends a long time."

Amie asked him how much he still owed on his place. He said, "I been a'paying on this pore little old place off and on for twenty years. The bank said we still owe seven hunnerd dollars. Hit don't look like me and the missus will ever own it a'fore we die."

They thanked him for what he had done and left. On the way they stopped at the county seat to visit the banker who held his mortgage. Amie said to Omie, "Ma, Grandpa owned that little piece of property, didn't he?"

"Yes, Amie, fer as I know. Why?"

"Ma, why don't we sell it for what we can get and pay his friends' mortgage?"

"Amie, do you mean it?"

"I do, Ma. We can start using some of our good fortune to help someone else."

"Amie, that shore would be a blessing to that poor old feller and his missus."

They talked to the banker and made a deal for the bank to take Omie's father's place as part payment on the mortgage they were holding on the old man's place. Amie paid the balance. When the deed was changed and notarized, the bank gave it to Amie.

Amie and Omie then went to the courthouse and recorded it. She then wrote a note and mailed the deed along with five hundred dollars. "I'll bet he will be surprised, Ma."

"I bet he will too, Amie. I shore am proud of you."

When they returned home, March was saddened by the news they brought back. "Shore wish the old feller could have come."

Amie broke in and said, "Pa, I want you and Ma to move into the big house with me."

March said, "Amie, we love you, and we sort of figured you might ask us to do that. We decided we would just as soon stay where we are. We ain't used to that kind of living and would feel better staying here. We hope you don't mind."

"Pa, you and Ma can live anywhere you want. I'll build you a new house, if you want one. Remember, on our way here in 1821? I said, one day I was going to be rich. We would go to Savannah and eat in all those fancy places and ride on those big ships. Well, I was just dreaming a child's dream then, but it has come true. We are going to do those things and more, until we get tired of doing them. I want you to hire an overseer to run this place. Then I want you to buy tickets on a ship from St. Marks to Savannah. Just as soon as you can find the right man to take over for you, we are going. While we are there, we'll find all of your folks and get them headed this way."

"Amie, that's a tall order. What will I do to keep busy if I hire someone to do my job?"

"Pa, you don't have to give up running El Destino. You will just be free to go when you want to."

"Well, I reckon if nothing else will do you, then I'll do it fer you. But just until we get through traveling."

"Pa, we aren't ever going to get through traveling, unless you and Ma want it that way."

March spent a considerable amount of time looking for a replacement. He finally decided on a man who was about thirty-five years old and who had been farming with his father all his life. March was satisfied this man knew "which end was up," as he put it.

Wade Noble was his name. March started right away and built another house for him. Then a date was set for him to come.

When he arrived in Monticello, March was there to meet him and brought him back to El Destino. When March introduced him to Amie, she looked into the bluest eyes she had ever seen. He was a rugged individual, tanned by long years in the sun. His hands were big and callused from hard work. He had a dazzling smile and a big cowlick in his hair.

Wade had a casual, easy way of talking. Amie was impressed with his knowledge and experience. He wasn't a braggart, she decided. He just stated what he could do in a simple and assuring manner. Amie decided he was going to make an excellent overseer.

They made their plans and set a sailing date. March bought their tickets. As the date for sailing approached, March intensified Wade's training.

The day before they were to sail March said to Amie, "I'm confident Wade can handle El Destino. We won't have to worry while we are gone."

They left early the next day. When they arrived in St. Marks their ship was ready to sail. The Gulf was calm, and sailing was a pleasure. When they rounded Florida through the Straits and entered the Atlantic, it was a rougher go.

Still they made good time and before they knew it, they were entering the Savannah River. Amie looked at her Mother and said, "Ma, I remember what you and Pa said when we were here before."

"What did we say?"

"You said one day we would be rich, and we would come back to Savannah with lots of money to spend. Pa said one day we would come back and eat in fancy cafes. I also made a vow that someday I would be rich and bring you and Pa here, and we would do all those things. All of our dreams have come true. We did come back!"

They didn't ride on "those ships" but did eat in "those fancy cafes" and stayed in the "finest hotels." Amie and her mother bought loads of things to take back with them to El Destino.

March did a lot of looking, but in the end, he said he didn't see anything he needed. They made arrangements to have all the things they had bought shipped to St. Marks. George would retrieve them when they arrived.

They left Savannah and traveled the same road that had brought them to Savannah so long ago. March wanted to visit with Jack if he was still at the same place. They were riding in a new buggy March had just purchased in Savannah, pulled by a matched pair of spirited horses that knew how to step. They were making record time.

March recognized the road that led to Jack's place and turned into it. When they reached the place Jack's house should have been, they found only the chimney standing. "It shore wasn't much when we were here, now it's all gone. I wonder what happened to Jack?" March worried aloud.

Omie said, "He shore was nice to us. I wish we could have seen him again. Maybe we could have helped him like we helped that old man in Kansas."

March turned the horses and started back the way they came saying, "I wanted to see him too. I wanted to thank him again fer that stew we ate. I remember, it shore was good. That's what I was thinking about when I killed that hog and nearly got eaten by a big old 'gator, remember?"

"We do, Pa. We won't ever forget. Ma and I were so worried that we might never see you again."

The first house they came to they inquired about Jack. They were told he had died a long time ago. Seemed he got too far from the house and couldn't get back. "I heered his dog a'barking in the swamp. When I went to see what he was a'barking at, I found Jack dead. He's been dead fer a long spell now!"

March mused to himself, "So many of the folks we knew are gone. We'd probably be gone too, if we had a'stayed in Caroline."

They hurried on and soon came to the old house where March "share cropped." The little shack they knew so well was still standing but leaned at a crazy angle.

March stopped the horses and let them drink from the spring from which the McCloud family had carried water so many years ago. Omie walked about with tears streaming from her eyes as old memories flooded back. Amie remembered too, but her memories were pleasant ones.

When the horses were rested, they resumed their trip. Just before dark they came to the house where March's oldest brother lived. When they drove into the yard, the dogs set up a yowling, alerting those inside.

A man came to the door and stood looking at them. Finally, he came closer and peered intently at March and said, "My God, is that you, March? You the last person in the whole dang world I would have expected. Y'all get down and come in. We was just setting down to supper. We ain't got a whole lot, but yore shore welcome to help us eat what we got. That's a mighty fancy rig you got there, March. I heered tell, you were a'doing well. Come on in the house and let the wife see you."

March said, "Tom, we need a place to stay for a day or two. Can you put us up?"

Tom replied, "March, we'll put you up, even if we have to sleep like we used to, three, or four to the bed. You remember?"

"I shore enough do, Tom."

Omie and Amie had already gone into the house. Inside Flora enthusiastically greeted them. She gave March a hug when he came in and asked, "March, can I fix you a bite to eat? Shorely you must be hongry as a bear."

"I shore am, Flora. I could eat a fried mule and an acre of collard greens."

"I see you ain't changed nary a bit, March."

March chuckled and asked, "Where are all the children?"

Tom answered, "March, you and Omie has been gone a long time; them chillen of ours are all growed up, and they got families of their own. Flora and me live by ourselves now."

Flora busied herself warming up leftovers for their supper. She said, sort of shame faced, "Same as always, ain't much to offer y'all."

March looked at Amie and Omie, then said to Tom, "Tom, we came to change all that."

"How's that, March? Y'all aiming to move in with us?" He said with a throaty laugh.

"No, something better than that. Tom, we have just come into a bunch of money. Well, not me, Amie has really. We want you and the rest of the family to come with us to El Destino and live."

"Why, shore, March, we'd just love to. Wouldn't we, Flora? And I reckon we can have a new buggy to ride in and some of them "high steppers" you are a'driving to pull it too?"

Amie spoke up and said, "Uncle Tom, it's true." She then told them the story of how she came to inherit all of Mr. Price's property.

Tom looked at them and said, "Good God Almighty, March. I thought y'all were a'funning me. I don't know. You know we ain't never been nowhere to speak of. The chillen ain't too fer from us neither. Good God, March, we's about to get this place paid fer. It ain't much, but hit'd be a little something we could leave for the young'uns when we die. March, I just don't know what to say."

"You don't have to say nothing right now. Think about it fer a day or two, then give us yore answer. Tomorrow I want you to go with us to see the rest of the family. We got the same proposition fer them."

They talked far into the night, catching up on old times and the happenings since March had left. Tom and Flora would just look at them and say, "Yore rich, March. I cain't believe it. Shore wish Ma and Pa could of a'knowed about hit. Wouldn't hit have been something, if they could of been here to help you spend some of hit? Wonder what the rest of them is a'gonna say? God Almighty, March, I just don't know."

Next day March and Tom visited other members of the family who lived nearby. They were invited to Tom's house the next day for a family reunion.

March told each of them what he had told Tom. Like Tom, they first thought March was teasing them. Finally, March was able to convince them he was serious. "Think over what I've said. When you come tomorrow, I'll expect yore answer." Two brothers were dead, but the offer was extended to their wives and children.

March's two sisters lived about a hundred miles away. March said he would visit them later. March was apprised of his sisters' affairs by Tom. Now he knew how to approach each of them.

When the families came together next day, the table held everything a body could desire in the way of food. Amie paid for it. The boys went into town and filled the wagon.

As they enjoyed the bountiful food, Amie had to repeat her story many times over, while all listened with wonder in their eyes. Tom was heard to exclaim time and again, "Good God, Almighty!"

At the end of the day no one was prepared to give March an answer. It was just too sudden, too much of a shock. When March first made the offer, they all said, "Dang right, we'll go! We'll be glad to leave this misery behind."

In the end they all said, "We'll have to study on it some."

March, Omie, and Amie left the next day to visit March's sisters. Before leaving March said, "We'll be back in a week. Y'all have yore minds made up and give us your answers."

When March found his sisters, he related the story of Amie's good fortune to them. He extended the same proposition to them he made to his brothers. His sisters also knew that March was the overseer on a huge plantation. They were proud for him too. Now this--it was more than they could believe!

They, like their brothers, would need time to talk it over with their husbands and children. As they talked, March made note of their financial status, and whether or not they owned their property, or if it was mortgaged. Amie suggested giving them Chemonie Plantation. They could all farm it together. "I don't reckon that would work, Amie. Better to help each one separately. That way, won't be no squabbling," March said.

"I reckon you're right, Pa."

In the end, only his two youngest brothers wanted to come with them. All the others said it was shore good of March to ask them, but they thought they would feel better staying and living the remainder of their lives in a familiar place.

March stayed long enough to ascertain each debt. Amie would then write a check to pay it off. For those who owned no property, a suitable parcel was found and purchased. Each one of March's family received a sum of money to ensure a good start, or for a nest egg.

When it was time to leave, they all came together for a final time. They thanked Amie for her generosity with tears of gratitude in their eyes and joy on their faces. March said to them once again, "My offer will always be open, if you ever want to come. Now then, Tom, you just come with us to Savannah. I'm giving this "fancy rig" to you."

Tom replied, "Good God Almighty, March."

When they arrived back in Savannah, March said he was going to buy a horse and ride to El Destino. He wanted to re-trace their old route and maybe see the people they had met along the way. They spent a few days seeing the sights and dining in the splendid restaurants. Omie and Amie bought additional clothing and furniture and shipped it to St. Marks.

March saw them safely aboard a ship sailing for New Orleans. It would visit St. Marks enroute to deposit Omie and Amie.

Tom and Flora were outfitted with new clothes and dined in all the fancy restaurants alongside March, Omie, and Amie. When March finally said goodbye to them, Tom and Flora were sitting in that "fancy rig" all decked out like Gentleman and Lady. As March rode away, he heard Tom shout, "Good God Almighty. Come up hosses!"

March set out to find their old trail. He camped at all the places they had camped before. He wanted to see as many of the people they had met before as possible.

He visited with the storekeeper, who still remembered trading with March for the panther skin.

March found the Parnells much the same as when they first met. Poor Mrs. Parnell still didn't have any snuff. When March left, he placed a hundred dollars on the bed with a note for her to get herself some snuff.

March rode and camped. The trail looked much the same as it did when the McCoud family traveled it, so long ago.

When he came to the place where Hawk had saved Omie's life, he was fearful his old friend Hawk would not be there. March worried within himself, "He's probably dead or gone to south Florida with the rest of his people. I hope he hasn't been captured and sent to Oklahoma."

March camped for two days, all the time remembering what Hawk had told him, "You ever come back, you camp here. Hawk will find you, if "Great Spirit" not come first."

From time to time, March fired his gun to let Hawk know that someone was there.

March was beginning to think the "Great Spirit" had already visited, when Hawk walked into camp just before dark. Hawk sat down as if March had been there all along and said, "Hawk think someday you come back. I keep watch. I glad see you again."

"Hawk, I'm shore glad to see you too! I was beginning to think the "Great Spirit" had got here first. We think of you often and the time you saved my Omie's life. I have had much good luck since I saw you. Now, I would like to repay you for what you did for us."

"Hawk not need for anything. Everything I need is there," he indicated with a sweep of his hand. "Hawk, old now; soon "Great Spirit" come for me. Hawk will see

Father, Mother, live same house. "Great Spirit" give Hawk much land. White man no take."

They smoked while they talked of the day when Omie was snake bitten. March cooked a meal, and Hawk shared it with him. They smoked again and talked into the night. Finally, they rolled into their blankets and slept.

The next morning Hawk said, "You come, stay with Hawk. I show you how he live."

"Hawk, I shore would like to spend a few days with you."

Hawk led the way deep into a large hammock where he had a palmetto shack in a clearing. He had a garden of pumpkins and squash. Hanging from a limb of a tree was a deer. Hawk said, "Must dry deer, or it spoil. Hawk need for winter."

"I'll help you."

Hawk cut the deer into thin slices while March built a fire. He placed the pieces of meat on poles and put them over the fire to dry slowly into hard, leathery pieces.

After two days, the meat was dried. Hawk placed it in a leather bag and hung it in his palmetto house. He said to March, "Now time for you, me, go hunting. Not far to lake. There, plenty fish, 'gator. You like eat 'gator?"

"Why, I reckon I do, Hawk. Ain't nothing that'll beat 'gator tail."

When they reached the lake, swarms of ducks took to the air. They settled again quickly when March and Hawk stopped moving. Hawk showed March where he set traps for fish. When Hawk picked up a trap, it was filled with fish. Hawk said, "Take some, turn rest loose. When Hawk come back, trap full again. Now, must find little 'gator, borrow tail."

As they slowly walked around the lake looking for an alligator to kill, March saw a large mound and asked Hawk what it was. Hawk replied, "That 'gator nest. Much eggs inside, soon hatch. Hawk have much 'gator tails."

"Let's take a look at it, Hawk. I ain't never seen one before."

"Must be careful. Mama 'gator not like."

March stood on top of the nest. Hawk explained it was made of leaves and rotting vegetation. "Get hot, make smoke, baby 'gator."

Suddenly, seemingly from out of nowhere, a huge alligator rushed upon them. March tried to run but tripped and fell. Mother 'gator, with huge jaws agape, sped toward him with a roar. March knew he would never be able to get to his feet in time to escape her. From the corner of his eye he saw Hawk coming with a broken limb.

Hawk arrived just as mother 'gator was about to take a bite from March. Hawk hit the 'gator on the head, and it stopped momentarily. With a roar, she turned on Hawk, jaws opened wide.

With a mighty swish of her tail, she broke Hawk's leg. Before March could get to his feet, she seized Hawk's foot in her mouth. Swiftly she began to roll over and over. Hawk's foot was torn from its socket.

March got to his feet and seized the limb Hawk had dropped. He began beating the 'gator with it. She turned Hawk's foot loose and backed off, mouth open, emitting loud hissing noises. March pulled Hawk away from the angry 'gator.

Hawk was bleeding profusely, his leg twisted out of joint at the hip. March made a tourniquet from his belt and put it around his leg to stop the bleeding.

March then carried him a safe distance before putting him down. Then he said, "Hawk, I'm mighty sorry about what happened to you. I'm going back to camp and will bring the horse to carry you back."

March hurried back to the campsite. He mounted his horse and returned as fast as the horse would run.

He helped Hawk on to the horse. Slowly they made their way back to camp. March helped him down and made him as comfortable as possible. "Hawk, you need a doctor to set that leg and do something to that stump. Do you know if there's a doctor near here?"

"Hawk not know doctor. Nearest person, maybe half day's walk."

"Where can I find this person?"

Hawk gave directions. March mounted his horse and said, "I'll be back as soon as I can."

When March found the house there was no one home. He decided to wait for a while. He sat down on the porch. About an hour later, a man appeared from the brush. He was startled to see March sitting on his porch.

March stood up and introduced himself and said, "My name is March McCloud. I need a doctor. My partner is hurt bad."

The man replied, "I ain't nary doctor. Fer as I know, there ain't no doctor here-bouts. What's the matter with yore friend?"

March decided the less he told the man the better. He quickly made up a story and said, "He broke his leg pretty bad and can't ride his horse. Do you have a wagon that you will sell to me?"

"Yeah, I got one, but hit's all I got. I can't sell it."

"Listen, I need a wagon to get my partner to a doctor, I'll pay whatever you ask." March could see the greed begin to grow in the man's eyes.

He said, "I just cain't hardly get along out here 'thout no wagon; I needs it too bad."

March knew the man had him over a barrel, so he said, "I'll make it worth yore while. You got anything to pull it with? If so, name me a price."

"I got a right smart pair of mules. Reckon there ain't none better in these parts. Reckon hit'd take a pretty piece of money fer me to let them go, seeing as how I'd have to go a fer piece to get another one."

"Just tell me what you want fer them," March said.

"I reckon I'd take four hunnerd fer the whole shebang."

March knew they weren't worth a third of that, but he had to have them. March counted out the money and gave it to him. "Help me hitch them up, and I'll be on my way."

March hurried back as fast as the mules would go. When he reached Hawk he found him with a high fever and writhing in pain. March loaded him into the wagon. He tied his horse to the rear and set off toward El Destino, some forty or fifty miles away.

He drove until the mules got tired or thirsty. Then, he would stop for a rest. March knew he had to avoid letting anyone know who his passenger was so he was unable to stop for help.

March drove for three days, stopping only long enough for the animals to rest and eat. While they were resting he tended Hawk and did a little cooking.

Hawk was awake but never made a sound or complained even though his leg was swollen to a hideous size. March wanted to stop in Madison or one of the other towns but was afraid that Hawk would be taken, and so he hurried on.

They arrived at El Destino just before midnight. March drove to the stable and hollered for Leroy.

Leroy answered, "Who dat out der?"

"It's March, Leroy. Light a lantern and get out here, and hurry up!"

Leroy came slowly from the stable rubbing his head to rid it of hay. March told him to saddle a horse and ride to Monticello for Dr. Jim. "Leroy, when Dr. Jim asks you what the trouble is, you just say you don't know. Tell him, I said for him to come at once and to be prepared for a broken leg and a missing foot. You got all that?"

"Yas, Suh, Marser Cloud. You knows that you can depend on Leroy. You say one his feets be's missing, Marser Cloud?"

"That's what I said. Now, ride like the devil was after you, and don't come back without Dr. Jim. Don't say a word to anyone other than him, all right?"

"Yas, Suh, Marser Cloud. I hears what you say. I's on de way. Get out de road, everybody; Leroy is on de move and ain't got no time for no foolishness!"

Leroy left with a clatter and soon the sound of his horse faded into the night. "I hope he don't kill hisself in the dark," March muttered.

March hurried to the house and woke Omie and told her what was happening. He had her prepare something to eat and a pot of coffee. He told her to bring it to the barn along with some quilts.

Then he went to the big house and woke Amie to let her know. "Omie's bringing some food and coffee. We'll be in the barn."

March next stopped at George's house and woke him. He told George to come as fast as he could to the barn. And he added, "On your way stop and get Mr. Noble."

As March rode away, George was standing in the doorway trying, without much success to put his pants on.

March dashed into the barn and threw some hay into an empty stall. He made it into a bed, then threw a horse blanket over it.

When George arrived, he quickly told him what was going on and warned him not to tell anyone. Then they unloaded Hawk from the wagon and brought him inside. They gingerly placed him on the makeshift bed. Hawk was awake, watching them but didn't make a sound while he was being moved.

Omie arrived with leftover biscuits and freshly brewed coffee. She fell to Hawk's side, hugging him and making him welcome.

A few minutes later, Amie arrived and did likewise. Omie served Hawk, George, Amie, and March some biscuits and hot coffee. As they ate, March told them all about the accident. They sat talking and drinking coffee while waiting for Jim to come.

March heard Wade coming and went outside to meet him. He told him what was happening and warned him not to say anything about what was going on. Omie heard the two men's conversation, and before they were inside the barn, she already had Wade poured a steaming cup of coffee.

Just before daybreak, they heard horses coming. Amie went to the door to see who it was. It was Jim and Leroy. As soon as Jim stepped down from his horse he wanted to know who he was supposed to treat. March quickly told him what had happened. He promised to explain it all later.

Jim brought in his bag and started to work on Hawk. He could see he had a badly broken leg, and his foot was missing. As he worked, he explained to Hawk what he was doing and tried to be as gentle as possible.

When he was ready to put the bones of Hawk's leg into place, he called for help. "I don't have anything for pain, March. Do you want to give Hawk some liquor?"

Hawk responded by saying, "Me no need for 'White Fire;' you not worry about Hawk."

When Jim was through, March cautioned Leroy and George once again not to tell anyone at all about their visitor.

They left George and Leroy to stay with Hawk. With Jim in tow, they went to the house for breakfast. Jim said, "March, I don't know how you got Hawk here without him bleeding to death. I might have to take that leg off at the knee later. It's a mess. Tell me what happened to him."

While they ate, March told them his story. He swore Jim to secrecy about Hawk. Jim assured March his secret was safe.

For several weeks, Jim continued to treat Hawk. Gradually his wounds healed. Omie and Amie nursed Hawk with wonderful care. After all, he was their true friend.

Jim announced one day, "I've done all I can for Hawk. He is going to need a crutch or something so that he can get about. Maybe we can fashion him a "peg" to walk on. I'll stop in again soon, and you can let me know what he wants to do."

March explained to Hawk what Jim had said about the peg, while he was recuperating. Hawk had seen another man with a peg and thought he might like one too. "I'll tell Doc and get you fixed up with one," March said.

March rode into town and told Jim what Hawk had said about the peg, and the very next day Jim brought a carpenter to make Hawk a peg. He spent a day cutting and fitting Hawk with a wooden leg. After several tries, Hawk mastered it and was able to take his first step since the alligator had bitten off his foot. Hawk made rapid progress and was soon able to get about with confidence.

It took some talking, but March convinced Hawk to stay at El Destino. He chose a site that seemed to satisfy Hawk and built a small house for him.

The location settled upon was several miles from the big house and well hidden near a swamp. March built a small corral and a barn for Hawk's horse. March had given him one of his best horses. They fenced and cleared a place for a small pasture so the horse could forage.

Every few days March rode to see that all was well with Hawk. He kept him well supplied. There was no need for Hawk to hunt or raise a garden.

March was confident that Hawk's new home was safe because George and Leroy were the only plantation workers who even knew Hawk was there.

Sometimes, in the cover of night, Hawk rode to the house and visited March. Mostly he was satisfied to stay in the deep woods riding wherever he went, owing to his crippled leg.

Several times, some of the work hands reported to March that they thought they saw someone riding through the woods. Once, one of them said he had seen tracks made by just one foot. The others had a great laugh at that, and one of the workers said, "How you gonna walk with jus' one feets?"

Chapter 22

One day Amie called all the slaves together and said to them, "I would like to set all of you free, but the other owners won't agree to let their people go. There is no place for you to go just now. Someday and, it may be soon, you will be set free. Until that happens, I'm going to make your life as good for you as I can. We are going to raise more hogs, more corn, and sugar cane. Each of you will have more time to tend your own garden. On Saturday and Sunday we'll rest. Only the animals will be cared for. I'm going to build you a church and see that you have a preacher. I intend to build a school for the children so they can learn to read and write. You will all be given lumber to repair your houses. Soon, we'll begin to build bigger and better ones. When the day comes that you are freed, I will give each of you some money if you choose to leave. That is all that I can do for you now. Please, be patient."

When March's two younger brothers arrived with their wives and children, March and Amie bought them small farms. They were supplied with mules and equipment and seeds for a start. March intended to see that they prospered before he ceased to help them.

Amie became silent partners with several business concerns. She demanded credit to be eased on the poor farmer. When they were unable to pay, she had their time extended or paid it for them. If one was in danger of losing his farm to the tax collector, she paid his taxes. No one ever knew she was involved.

Life at El Destino returned to its former days of glory. The great house once again was lighted. Sounds of music poured from the windows far into the night.

This time it wasn't a minuet or a waltz played on the violin. It was a fiddle and bow, the ring of the banjo, as brogans dragged across the floor and men buck danced, or ladies and gents clogged. The caller intoned, "Grab your partner and bring her to the floor; circle to the left and couple up four. Now, everybody, swing your partner."

Just a bunch of farmers, you say?

Yes, and more. Bankers and lawyers, doctors, Senators, and the Governor, too. Yes, lights and music chased the gloom and darkness from the great house, restoring it once again to its former glory.

Amie too, regained her place as the most popular girl in Jefferson and Leon Counties. Invitations no longer were sent to just the rich. Amie welcomed everyone, rich and poor alike to El Destino. She was loved and adored by all.

The black folks still didn't come into the house, but they gathered near the open windows. They laughed at the white folks, and the white folks laughed back. They mastered the waltz and the fox trot, dancing barefoot in the sand. They excelled at buck dancing and clogging. They shared the food from the heavily laden tables.

Funny how folksy ways caught on and became the rage after Amie became the Master of El Destino.

The black folks had their church, and it was preaching, praying, and singing all day Saturday and

Sunday. At night, from their new houses came the sound of laughter.

In the fields it was a chant to keep the rhythm of work. At odd moments someone would stop work and break into a mournful spiritual about "Moses" or "Zek'ul" or "De Lawd."

Life was bearable when hope glimmered, and it radiated from Miss Amie. Hope was rapidly becoming highly contagious.

The years slipped swiftly away. March and Omie became old and stricken in their bodies. They never moved into the big house but chose to live as they always had---simply.

They didn't mind others living that way. When a dance was held, they would join in. Both March and Omie could still step pretty lively. Most of the time though, they sat in their rocking chairs drawn up near the musicians and rocked their grandchildren.

"Hold these young'uns, Grandpa, while Amie and I show these city folks how a buck dance ought to be done," Wade would often say. Then, Wade and Amie would rock the great house.

March said to his grandchildren, "Look, there at the window, ain't that an Indian I see?"

"No, Grandpa, there aren't any Indians at El Destino."

"Don't be so sure about that."

"Oh, Grandpa!"

Do-si-do. Now, swing that pretty gal around the floor.

Postscript

In 1828, El Destino was owned by John Nutall. He sold it to his brother, William B. Nutall, in 1832, for the princely sum of seventeen thousand dollars.

John Nutall then purchased land just inside Taylor County. There the Aucilla River disappears into a "sinkhole" near Goose Pasture. It re-appears astride the Jefferson/Taylor County line at a place known as Nutall Rise, obviously named for the owner of the land.

In 1860, George Noble Jones, purchased El Destino from William B. Nutall. When the Civil War between the states began it was essentially about slavery. The slaves were eventually freed, including those of El Destino Plantation.

Mr. Whitehouse purchased the property around the turn of the century. El Destino flourished while other plantations slowly diminished from the lack of workers.

It remained in the Whitehouse family until 1991, when the heirs offered El Destino property for sale in parcels. I bought 31 acres bordering U.S. Highway 27 and Old St. Augustine Road, (the original trace running east from St. Augustine to Pensacola in the extreme western part of Florida). My wife, Betty, and I built a house overlooking the entire 31 acres.

Great plantations were broken up and sold in small parcels. Some were returned to their natural state as owners abandoned them using them only for vacation and hunting lodges. A few were seized for back taxes and sold piecemeal or became a ward of the county or state.

Many great plantations remain until this day, scattered in north Florida and south Georgia. Most are not working farms. Mainly they are used for private hunting preserves and vacation homes for the wealthy. The primary motive, I suspect, is for tax shelters.

The story I wrote is fiction, of course, but much of it is historically correct. All the things I wrote about were the norm for that period and even until the late 1940s.

Arrowheads I found that were lost by the Indians, and old plows I unearthed that were handmade from the forge at El Destino spawned the idea for this novel.

I have chosen to think Miss Amie would have done the following:

She freed the slaves at El Destino. She gave those who chose to leave money. For those who wanted to remain she paid fair wages for their work. She also gave those who stayed at El Destino a small acreage and built houses for them. They were free to leave anytime they desired.

El Destino was a real place. It has had a long history; some unsavory, I am sure. Until recently the land was unchanged. If the real characters, who are mimicked by my imaginary ones, could come back today they would discover the face of the land changed very little.

About The Author

Clayton Martin is retired from the United States Air Force and lives on 31 acres of the former historic El Destino plantation near Tallahassee, Florida with his wife Betty. Several of his stories have been published in the *Florida Wildlife* magazine. From his front porch observations come most of his inspirations. He has several books of short stories and another novel that will be published very soon.

Books Published:
    El Destino (The Destination)
    When Chickens Had Long Legs

If your local bookstore is out of stock, copies may be obtained by going to www.firstpublish.com.

Books are available at special discounts when purchased in bulk for premiums and sales promotions as well as for fund raising or educational use. Special editions or excerpts can also be created to specification. For details, contact Customer Service at the address below.

FirstPublish, Inc.
300 Sunport Lane
Orlando, FL 32809
888-707-7634

Books may be ordered directly from the author by sending cash, check, or money order in the amount of:

$16.95 for *El Destino (The Destination)*
-or-
$14.95 for *When Chickens Had Long Legs*

To: Clayton M. Martin
5552 St. Augustine Rd.
Monticello, FL 32344-6841
(Allow up to three (3) weeks for delivery.)
Email comments to: martinc@hcsmail.com